Jed Sabbides...

She watched in st
lithe strides he wa   n
front of her.

"Phoebe, this is a s
but the child threw
you Mom."

His baritone greeting set every nerve in her
body on edge, and she could do nothing about
the sudden leap in her pulse. Steeling herself to
remain calm, she glanced up at him and politely
said "Hello, Jed," conscious of her son at her side.

"I wasn't aware you had a child. Nobody told me."
Jed's piercing black gaze sliced through her like a
knife, and she had never seen such rage—quickly
controlled as he turned his attention to her son.

"Hello, young man. I heard you telling your mom
you liked my car." He smiled down at Ben. "Would
you like to see inside? Or I have a better idea—
let's go for a drive."

"No," Phoebe snapped, tugging Ben closer to
her side. "He knows he must never get into a
stranger's car." She wished he had not yelled mom
quite so loud—not that it would have made much
difference.

Jed turned his head and stared down at her, and
the look in his eyes made her blood freeze.

"Admirable. But you and I are not strangers,
Phoebe, so there is no harm in introducing me to
your son—is there?" he queried silkily.

All about the author...
Jacqueline Baird

JACQUELINE BAIRD was born and brought up in Northumbria, U.K. She met her husband when she was eighteen. Eight years later, after many adventures around the world, she came home and married him. They still live in Northumbria and now have two grown-up sons.

Jacqueline's number-one passion is writing. She has always been an avid reader and she had her first success as a writer at the age of eleven, when she won first prize in the Nature Diary of the Year competition at school. But she always felt a little guilty because her diary was more fiction than fact.

She always loved romance novels and when her sons went to school all day, she thought she would try writing one. She's been writing for the Harlequin® Presents line ever since, and she still gets a thrill every time a new book is published.

When Jacqueline is not busy writing, she likes to spend her time traveling, reading and playing cards. She was a keen sailor until a knee injury ended her sailing days, but she still enjoys swimming in the sea when the weather allows.

She visits a gym three times a week and has made the surprising discovery that she gets some good ideas while doing the mind-numbingly boring exercises on the cycling and weight machines.

Jacqueline Baird

THE SABBIDES
SECRET BABY

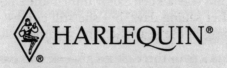

HARLEQUIN®

TORONTO • NEW YORK • LONDON
AMSTERDAM • PARIS • SYDNEY • HAMBURG
STOCKHOLM • ATHENS • TOKYO • MILAN • MADRID
PRAGUE • WARSAW • BUDAPEST • AUCKLAND

Recycling programs
for this product may
not exist in your area.

ISBN-13: 978-0-373-12955-3

THE SABBIDES SECRET BABY

First North American Publication 2010.

Copyright © 2010 by Jacqueline Baird.

www.eHarlequin.com

Printed in U.S.A.

THE SABBIDES
SECRET BABY

CHAPTER ONE

JED SABBIDES shifted restlessly in his seat. The plane was beginning its descent, and not before time. A certain part of his anatomy was stirring at the thought of the delectable Phoebe waiting for him in London. He had planned to be in New York for three weeks, but had cut short his trip by a day and rearranged his schedule to work from the London office tomorrow to get back to her.

He had to be in Greece by Saturday evening for his father's birthday, and with the level of frustration he was feeling he had decided after a business lunch that only one night with Phoebe was not going to be enough... A couple of telephone calls and the Sabbides company jet had been waiting for him at Kennedy Airport—the five-hour time difference between the two continents was for once a blessing.

A frown marred his broad brow. When had he *ever* changed his schedule for a woman? Never... The answer made him slightly uneasy, and his thoughts drifted back to the first time he had met Phoebe...

Exiting the elevator on the ground floor of the hotel he was staying at while he assessed the place with a view to purchase, Jed glanced at the girl walking across the foyer and paused for a moment, his dark eyes lingering in appreciation on her feminine form.

She was about five-eight, with pale blonde hair that fell in soft waves to her slender shoulders. Her profile was exquisite, and the sombre black skirt and white shirt she wore did nothing to distract from her shapely figure as she seemed to glide across the marble floor on a pair of legs that would make any red-blooded male's imagination go into overdrive.

His arrested gaze followed her as she stepped behind the reception desk and then turned with a smile for an approaching guest. Her smile took his breath away. His attraction was instant, and shockingly physical. He was without a woman at the time, and in that moment he decided the girl was going to be his, not for a second contemplating failure.

He approached the reception desk and asked if she could recommend a good restaurant. She tilted back her head, the better to look at him, and he realised she was even more beautiful up close. His fascinated gaze took in the delicate lines of her oval-shaped face—the creamy skin, the full mouth, and the brilliant blue eyes that now met his. He smiled and held her gaze, and her eyes widened in instinctive female recognition of his masculine interest. She actually blushed. Later he would learn why she did that.

Phoebe in the Greek language meant shining, brilliant, and she was all that and more—beautiful with a perfect body and a quick mind.

He asked her to have dinner with him that night. Amazingly she refused, stating she was not allowed to date guests, but he charmed her into telling him she only worked there at weekends to supplement her income while studying Politics and History at University.

He duly checked out, returning the next day to ask Phoebe again for a date and she agreed.

He had never met a woman yet who had turned him down—usually they chased him—and it was a novel experience, having to wait over a month before he got her into bed.

Mainly because Phoebe shared a house with three other students—two girls Kay and Liz, and the third a guy called John—she had virtually no privacy. But she flatly refused to dine with Jed in the suite he kept in one of the family-owned London hotels. Her excuse was that she would feel uncomfortable, having seen the kind of women who accompanied men to their rooms for only a few hours in the hotel where she worked.

She was a few weeks short of twenty-one, and her youth worried him a little. He could not decide if her concern was genuine modesty or if, like most women, she was angling for more than he was prepared to offer.

It was sheer coincidence, when entering the Empire Casino in the heart of London one night after Phoebe had left him frustrated yet again, that he met an old poker buddy of his and found the solution to his problem. The man had just been knocked out of the World Serious Poker Tournament, which was taking place in the casino at the time, and over a drink told him he was going to America and wanted someone to caretake his London apartment and his cat Marty while he was away.

Casually Jed told Phoebe the story, and asked if she was interested in the job. He introduced her to his friend, and when the cat purred and wrapped itself around her ankles she agreed.

It was a win-win situation all round, and finally Jed got further than a goodnight kiss. But even then she kept him waiting another few days!

It was a coincidentally novel solution, and a bit devious, he knew—but Jed was a cynic where the female of the species was concerned, and knew it was well worth the wait.

Pheobe surprised him—she was actually a virgin, a first for him—but amazingly she was the most eager and most incredibly responsive lover he had ever had...

That had been twelve months ago, he suddenly realised— another first for him. He had never kept a lover so long in all his thirty years.

With his experience of women he had long ago realised wealth was his main attraction to any female, and given his father was now married for the fourth time it was hardly surprising.

Not that it mattered to Jed. By the age of twenty-five he'd become a multi-millionaire in his own right—courtesy of the internet at first, as a student at university having played poker on line, and then he had moved on to trading on the financial markets. Essentially another form of gambling, but one that made better use of his brilliant mind. He'd set up his own company, JS Investments, and never looked back.

At his father's request he had agreed to join the family firm while keeping on with his own business, and had soon virtually taken over the running of the Sabbides Corporation, which had for decades specialised in hotels as well as other areas of the leisure industry. The company was now incredibly successful, but Jed's relationship with his father—always strained—had become increasingly bad.

If his father had taught Jed anything it was that marriage was not for him, and he kept his sex-life strictly separate from his business and family. No relationship lasted more than a few months—eight had been the longest until Phoebe. He certainly didn't believe in marriage, and he had told Phoebe most explicitly at the start. She had laughed at him and told him marriage was the last thing on her mind. She was determined to get a good degree, then start her career and hopefully travel the world.

On their first date, when she had asked what he did, he had simply said he was a businessman and travelled between offices in London, Athens and New York. But later her friend Liz had told her that mentions in the press referred to him as a 'Greek Tycoon'—a description he abhorred.

Yet it did not seem to influence Phoebe at all. In the time they had been together she had never hinted at commitment, never asked him for anything, and he was pretty sure she had no hidden agenda. He had nothing to worry about. One year or two, as long as the passion lasted Phoebe was his.

Seven weeks ago she had completed her degree, and the graduation ceremony had been last week. She had invited him to attend and told him her aunt was coming as well. He avoided meeting members of his women-friends' family if possible, and had said he would try to make it. As he'd been in New York at the time he'd had the perfect excuse not to go...

He had called Phoebe on the morning of the ceremony and wished her luck. She had been fine—especially after he'd mentioned he had a special surprise for her. Maybe she wasn't *so* different from the other women he had known, he thought cynically.

He often bought her gifts, and she was grateful and showed it in bed. This time he had bought her a spectacular diamond necklace—because if he was honest he did feel slightly guilty at missing her graduation. And now he was a day early, which he knew without conceit would please Phoebe.

The thought made him smile in a way that was all male sensual anticipation…

The plane landed and Jed stood up, shrugged on his jacket and straightened his tie. Tall, broad-shouldered, dark-haired and strikingly attractive, he was the epitome of the super-rich successful alpha male. He picked up his laptop and, with a goodbye to the smiling flight attendant, exited the aircraft.

Phoebe turned off the shower and stepped out of the cubicle. It was nine in the evening, and she wanted an early night so she would be totally rested and ready for Jed's arrival tomorrow night.

Her stomach fluttered at the thought…

She glanced at her reflection in the mirrored wall as she reached for a bath sheet from the towel rail to wrap around her slender body. Slender for how much longer? she wondered, with a growing sense of elation tinged with slight concern.

She had yet to tell her boyfriend Jed she was pregnant…

Jed Sabbides was a successful financier, and also the power behind the throne of the Sabbides Corporation. Phoebe had suspected from the beginning that he was wealthy, simply by his supremely confident attitude—which was why at first she had been wary of him. He'd seemed so far out of her league, but now she was hopelessly in love for the first time in her life. Her flatmate Liz had told her the full extent of his mind-boggling wealth, at the same time as she'd tried to warn Phoebe—after she'd been offered the job of taking care of this apartment last summer—that Jed was setting her up to be nothing more than his live-in lover in London...

Liz had been proved wrong...

True, within days of her moving into this apartment they had become lovers, but they did *not* live together...

Jed respected her, and stayed at a permanent suite at a deluxe hotel the Sabbides Corporation owned when working in London, while having an apartment on her own had allowed Phoebe to study hard in her final year at university.

Despite Jed's wealth they were just like any other couple in love, she told herself. They occasionally went out to dinner, or a film, and after their relationship had become intimate he'd often stayed overnight—if pressure of work allowed, sometimes more than one night. Jed had left a few items of clothing here over the year, but he definitely did not live here. He travelled a lot—as Phoebe knew to her cost when she lay aching for him in the big bed at night—but she had the compensation of the ginger cat Marty to keep her company when he was gone.

Jed rarely discussed business with her, but it had not taken her many months to realise he was a workaholic and split his time between two continents. But on the bright side he had once told her he had an older sister, who was married with two young girls whom he adored, so he obviously liked children—a positive sign, surely. He would want their baby just as much as she did, she was convinced...

Phoebe had met Jed when he was a guest at the hotel where she'd worked as a receptionist, and her life had changed from that moment. She had glanced up at the sound of his deep, slightly accented voice, looked into his gleaming dark eyes and been transfixed. He was the most gorgeous man she had ever seen. Then he had smiled at her, and every nerve in her body had tingled with an excitement she had never felt before. Incapable of looking away, she had blushed scarlet.

Twelve months later the sight of him and the sound of his voice still excited her beyond belief—and sometimes still made her blush…

Phoebe Brown—maybe soon Phoebe Sabbides, she thought, lost in a daydream of the future. Snagging a handtowel from the rail, she bent her head and began to towel-dry her hair.

'Aghh!' she yelled, blinded by the towel as a large hand grasped her bare shoulder. 'What the heck?' she exclaimed as she was spun round and held at arm's length.

The towel fell from her hands, her hair forgotten, as she looked up at Jed, her heart leaping in her chest. Tall, dark and handsome did not do him justice—he was so much more than that. He had a dynamic vitality about him—a presence that drew the eye of men and women alike wherever he went—especially the woman. And why not? Phoebe thought, eagerly drinking in the sight of him. He was magnificent.

'Jed—it is you.'

'I should hope so.' He grinned down at her. 'Who else would you welcome in your bathroom?' he mocked.

Then his hands slipped from her shoulders to unwrap the towel from her body, his laughing eyes darkening as they roamed hungrily over her shapely form.

'Now, this—this is what I have dreamed of for weeks.' His gaze lingered on the proud thrust of her full breasts, the rose-tipped nipples tightening beneath his gaze. 'But the reality exceeds my wildest dreams.'

Phoebe tilted her head back further. He had shed his jacket and tie and unfastened the first few buttons of his shirt, revealing the tanned column of his throat and a hint of black curling body hair. A slow, appreciative smile parted her full lips.

'Ah, Jed… I've missed you so much.' She sighed, and was gathered into his arms. His dark head dipped and his mouth covered hers. She wrapped her arms around his neck and they kissed with all the pent-up hunger and need that had built up over the time they had been apart.

His hands stroked down her back, and when they had to break for breath his head dipped lower, to capture one pert nipple into the heat of his mouth, licking and suckling as he tipped her backwards over a strong arm and delivered the same incredible pleasure to its partner.

'Damn, Phoebe, I can't wait,' he groaned.

She ran a hand through his thick hair and slid the other through the opening of his shirt, desperate to feel again the warmth of his bronzed skin and the pebble-like nipples half hidden in crisp curls. She saw the flush over his high cheekbones, the gleaming brown eyes deep black pools of desire, and she stroked her hand lower. Her fingers traced the rock-hard outline of his arousal through the fabric of his pants and she knew exactly what he meant.

Neither could she… It was the longest they had been apart since they had met, and the liquid heat between her thighs was a potent testament of her need of him.

Catching her hand, he thrust it away and, pinning her against the wall, unzipped his pants to free his straining length. Then he was lifting her high, cupping her buttocks, and she locked her legs around his back as he thrust into her moist feminine core.

They came together in a frenzied passion.

Phoebe's hands clasped behind his neck as she welcomed his hungry possession, her body pulsing as he plunged fast and furious, deeper and deeper, until she felt herself quivering on the brink of an ecstasy her body was screaming out for. With one last ferocious thrust he drove them both over the edge into a tumultuous climax.

Her head fell into the curve of his neck, her slender body shuddering in the aftermath of release. She could feel the heavy pounding of his heart against her own, and for a long moment she was incapable of movement.

'Forgive me, Phoebe.' She heard the rasping tone of his voice, and, lifting her head, she looked into his dark smouldering eyes. 'But I needed you so badly.'

'Me too,' she murmured as he brushed his lips gently against hers and lowered her slowly down his long body.

He steadied her with an arm around her slender waist as her legs wobbled a little. 'Are you sure you are okay?'

'Better now. I only have to look at you to want you,' she admitted freely, ecstatic at his unexpected early arrival.

'Then keep that thought while I get out of these clothes,' he said, with a wry glance at his pants around his knees before stepping out of them.

Phoebe bent down, intending to pick up the bath sheet from the floor, but Jed caught her wrist and pulled her upright.

'Don't bother,' he drawled giving her a sensuous smile. 'You won't need it for what I have planned next.' And as she watched he stripped off the remainder of his clothes.

Phoebe could not help it—he was her very own Greek god, she thought, excitement stirring inside her all over again as she let her eyes roam freely over him.

Jed her lover was six feet three of sheer perfection. His hair was black and slightly curly, and at the moment sexily dishevelled by her eager hands. His eyes were a golden-brown that darkened in passion to jet-black—as she knew only too well—and his nose was a straight blade in the fabulous structure of his handsome face. His sensual mouth

was wide, the lips perfectly etched—the bottom slightly
fuller than the top—and his jaw was square.

She could look at his face for ever, but the temptation
of his wide shoulders and the smooth bronzed skin was
becoming too much, and her gazed dropped to his broad
chest and the dusting of black body hair that drew the eye
down again over the well-defined muscles of his stomach,
narrow waist, lean hips and long, long legs. He was all
muscle and sinew, without an inch of fat on his impressive
frame. As for his manhood, amazingly raising again from
between his strong thighs, it fascinated her—Jed fascinated
her, full-stop...

'Like what you see?' he quipped, and swiftly she raised
her eyes to his. Even now, after all this time, she blushed
at having been caught staring.

'Yes.' Like? She *loved* him—and maybe now was the
time to tell him her news. But before she could find the
words he swept her off her feet and carried her into the
bedroom.

'Wait, Jed—don't you want a drink or something to eat
after your journey? And why are you here a night early?'

'Because I could not wait another day, and all I want to
eat is you.' Laying her down on the bed, he stretched out
beside her.

Thrilled at his need for her, she reached for him—and
what followed was a night like no other. He made love to
her with an achingly slow passion that drove her wild with
excitement, exploring every curve and crevasse, seducing
all her senses as he drove her to climax. As for Phoebe it
was as if she was possessed by some other entity, and any
faint, lingering sexual inhibitions she'd had vanished as she
explored every inch of him. He encouraged her with hands
and mouth, teeth and tongue, and led her deeper along a
path of ever more inventive sex, driving her to heights she

had never reached before over and over again. It was if he could not get enough of her, nor she of him.

Finally, hours later, lying exhausted in the crook of his arm but unable to sleep, her mind spinning with disjointed thoughts, she looked across at his beloved face and wondered if their child would look like him. Then she wondered if his returning early was the special surprise he had promised, and frowned. Stupid, but she had secretly been nursing the hope that it might be a ring. In her fantasy scenario she had imagined him asking her to marry him before she told him she was pregnant.

'I can hear you thinking, Phoebe—what's wrong?' Jed's deep voice rumbled.

Leaning up, she spread her hand across his chest and stared down into his slumberous dark eyes. 'Nothing. I was just wondering if coming back early was the surprise you promised me. I have to say if so it was the best ever.' And, dipping her head, she kissed him.

'I aim to please—but, no.' Rolling her onto her back, he slid off the bed and switched on the light. 'Stay where you are. I'll be back in a minute,' he said.

She watched him stroll naked out of the bedroom, to return a minute later with a black leather box in his hand.

'Sit up, Phoebe.' And she did.

'For your graduation from university.' He opened the box to reveal a dazzling platinum and diamond necklace. Slipping it around her neck, he fastened it. Then, running his hands over her slender shoulders and down to cup her breast, he added, 'And also for your graduation in the bedroom.' He rolled her nipples between his fingers. 'I didn't think sex could get any better, but I surprised myself. And you were with me all the way, surprising me even more, my incredibly wanton woman.'

'Thank you, Jed,' she murmured. 'The necklace is breathtaking.'

She looked down at the dazzling cascade of gems around her throat, not wanting to reveal the slight disappointment she felt. But as she glanced lower, at his long tanned fingers teasing her breasts, it wasn't disappointment she experienced but a renewed surge of arousal in what she had thought was her exhausted body.

Reaching up to wrap her arms around his neck, she brushed his lips with hers. 'And I love you,' she said softly.

She had told him enough times before, but it suddenly struck her that Jed had never actually said the words to her in English. He'd said she was beautiful and that he loved her body, he had told her so many times, and she had assumed he had said I love you in Greek, which was the language he used in the throes of passion. Now she was not so confident...

Telling herself not to be so silly—after what they had just done she was no longer the blushing innocent, that was for sure—she straddled his great body and, taking control, made love to him with a powerful passion which finally exhausted them both.

Phoebe awoke to feel a large male hand cupping her breast and the unmistakable pressure of an aroused male against her bum. A husky voice was murmuring in her ear, 'Ah, Phoebe, you feel so good.'

She stretched sinuously, and groaned her pleasure as Jed's other hand stroked around her waist to settle on her tummy, his long fingers edging to the curls at the apex of her thighs.

But her stomach had ideas of its own, and it wasn't *settled* at all. In a flurry of arms and legs she slid off the bed and dashed towards the bathroom.

'What the hell, Phoebe?' She heard Jed swear.

Unable to answer him she dashed inside, closing the door behind her, and turned on the tap of the vanity unit. Maybe a drink of water would stop her need to heave. But it was no use, and two seconds later she was on her knees retching in the toilet but with surprisingly little result!

Slowly she straightened, and after flushing the toilet she turned to splash her face with water and wash her mouth out. Maybe she was not going to be cursed with morning sickness after all. Maybe if she learnt to lie still or move with more care the urge to be sick would be averted, she pondered, eyeing her reflection in the mirrored door of the floor-to-ceiling cabinet.

Her full lips curved in a feminine smile. She did not look any different yet. She simply looked like a very well-loved woman, and the marks of passion on her breast and thighs were evidence of the fact—along with the diamond necklace that adorned her throat. She sighed happily. When she would ever wear it she had no idea, but it was a fantastic present, and the night had been incredible. Jed had proved in a dozen different ways how much he wanted her—including a couple she had never experienced before. But now she recognised that between lovers even the unimaginable was acceptable and exquisitely pleasurable.

'Phoebe?'

She heard him call her name.

Now was as good a time as any to tell him she was pregnant, she decided—with her confidence sky-high. 'Coming in a minute,' she called back and, taking a towel from the cupboard, she wrapped it around her naked body before exiting the bathroom.

'What took you so long?' he drawled, the eyes that met hers gleaming with humour and undisguised desire.

Her gaze swept over his lean muscled body splayed

across the bed, over the sleek golden skin with its subtle pattern of black hair in strategic places, and noted he was still mightily aroused. He lifted a long fingered hand and beckoned her to join him, and her heart turned over.

'I'm waiting for my morning sex,' he said with an anticipatory grin.

A sensual shiver slid down her spine. He wanted her. Jed loved her—she could see it in his eyes.

Taking a step towards him, she grinned back. 'And *I* am pregnant, and thought I was going to be sick.' She saw the anticipation fade from his eyes. 'But don't worry—I'm fine now,' she told him swiftly as she reached the bed.

A certain part of his anatomy had faded equally fast, she registered as he swung his legs over the other side of the bed and stood up. 'Jed?' she began, and stopped as he turned to face her, shocked by the flash of violent anger she caught in his eyes before, as if a shutter had fallen his handsome face became devoid of all expression.

He stared at her for a long moment, and the transformation from eager lover to cold hard stranger could not have been more obvious. She shivered again—but this time with a deep sense of foreboding.

CHAPTER TWO

PREGNANT. Phoebe was pregnant. It wasn't possible. He had taken every possible precaution—but had she? Jed asked himself the question, and a red mist of rage engulfed him as his totally panicked brain scrambled for an acceptable answer. Counting to ten didn't work. He got up to a thousand before he reached the glaringly obvious conclusion and finally trusted himself to turn and speak to her without yelling.

'I'm sure you *think* you are fine,' he drawled with biting cynicism, while battling to keep a lid on the fury still simmering inside him and retain his legendary cool control. 'Standing there with diamonds around your elegant neck, and according to you pregnant with what I presume you are going to claim is *my* child.'

He could not believe he had been suckered in by Phoebe's so-called innocence; she was like all the rest—if not worse—because she had succeeded where other women had failed with the oldest trick in the book.

'Of course the baby is yours.'

He heard the shock in her voice but ignored it.

'You know you are the only man I have ever made love with. I love you, and I thought you loved me.'

'You thought wrong. I don't *do* love—don't believe in the concept.'

'Why are you being like this?' She looked at him with wide puzzled eyes.

'Why? Because I have no wish to be tricked into becoming a father,' he drawled sardonically. 'Cast your mind back to the beginning. I always used protection. You then suggested going on the pill and I—more fool me—because of your initial innocence was tempted by the idea of condom-free sex for the first time in my life. I introduced you to my own private Dr Marcus, and he supplied your birth control pills. You did not even have to remember to collect them as he arranged for them to be delivered to you here. So there could have been no missed prescription, no mistake—so tell me, when did this conception occur?'

Whatever reaction Phoebe had expected, this sneering, cynical hard-eyed stranger standing facing her bore no resemblance to the Jed she'd thought she knew and loved. Her emotions were frozen in shock and she simply stated the truth.

'The weekend in Paris. I forgot to take my pills with me.'

'I might have guessed.' Jed's analytical mind, no longer blinded by sex, put two and two together and instantly saw through Phoebe's devious plan.

'I remember the only time you argued with me instead of being the eager lover was when I returned from spending Easter in Greece. You complained I never took you abroad with me, and moaned that the only time you had been out of the country was a day-trip to Belgium. You had not even been to Paris, so I took you there. Now you expect me to believe you mistakenly left your pills behind and never thought to mention the fact in the three days we stayed? How very convenient for you,' he drawled mockingly. 'That was the end of April, and now it is the beginning of July—you must be two months pregnant.'

'Nine weeks,' she amended softly. Maybe it was just shock making Jed behave like the biggest louse on the planet, Phoebe rationalized.

'What took you so long to tell me? Don't answer that—let me guess. You waited until you had finished your exams and graduated, but you never had any intention of starting a career other than living in the lap of luxury at my expense. You're a highly intelligent woman, Phoebe, and your timing is perfect. But no one takes me for a fool, and if your unusually spectacular and wanton display in bed last night was supposed to soften me up to get me to marry you are out of luck. No man expects his mistress to get pregnant.'

Through the fog of numbness Phoebe was devastated that he could actually believe she was so conniving as to have executed the plan he had formed in his mind. As for calling her his mistress—that was the last straw.

'I was never your mistress—I would never be any man's mistress. I thought you were my boyfriend. I thought you—'

He cut her off.

'Come off it, Phoebe, don't pretend you are that naïve. I got this apartment for you.'

'I thought I was housesitting for your friend and Marty.'

'You were—but he sold me the place three months after he left and said you could keep the cat. Apparently he has found a different kind of feline to snuggle up to—hopefully one less devious than you.'

'Devious!' she cried 'How can you call me that after all we have shared?'

'Quite easily. I gave you a car, jewels, clothes—whatever you wanted you could have. But a wedding ring was never on offer, and you knew that perfectly well from the start and agreed with me. If you think for one minute you can trap me with a child that was never on my agenda...think again.'

Phoebe sank down onto the bed, her mind in turmoil. He had said a child was not on his agenda. Typical business-speak, she realized, for what he really meant. He did not want their child and it was like a knife to her heart. She could not bear to look at Jed, and took a few deep, steady-ing breaths. Then finally the import of his disavowal of love as a concept registered in her mind, and in a flash of blinding clarity she saw she had been deluding herself from the very start of their relationship. While she had fallen in love and thought Jed was her boyfriend he had only considered her his mistress and treated her accordingly.

Now a lot of little niggling things over the past year made sense. No wonder he had never suggested she go to Greece with him and meet his family and friends, or go anywhere else with him on his travels. He had always had some excuse for not being around when her Aunt Jemma came up from Dorset to London to see her, and she had asked him often enough.

Jed had wined, dined and bedded her. He had even given her a car a week before Christmas. She had tried to refuse, saying he was too generous, but he had insisted she take the car, saying it would be useful for driving home for the holiday. He hadn't been able to spend it with her because he always went to Greece for the festive season. Much in the same way he'd insisted when he gave her a jewelled clip six weeks after they met, then a diamond bracelet for her twenty-first last August, and insisted on taking her shopping for designer clothes and lingerie that were not really her.

She had learnt it was easier to accept gracefully than to object. But she had never met any of his friends other than the man who had originally owned this apartment, and Dr Marcus with whom he had gone to school. She was simply his mistress in London. The weekend in Paris had been the only time he had taken her abroad—what a cliché! Then another sickening thought hit her. If he considered her simply a mistress maybe she was not the only one. He probably had others in New York and Greece and heaven knew where else.

Her shoulders slumped and her head fell forward. She raised her hands to run them despairingly through her tangled hair, blinking away the tears that threatened. How could she have been so dumb, so mistaken about Jed, her first and only lover?

Liz had been right all along, and she had been too besotted to see the truth...

Jed looked at Phoebe's downbent head saw the utter devastation she could not hide. The shock and anger that had overtaken him subsided a little. If she was pregnant of course he would take care of her. But first he needed Dr Marcus to confirm the pregnancy and, given he had been away for weeks at a time throughout their affair, he needed to be certain the child was his before he could even consider marrying her—though no child of his was going to be born out of wedlock. *Lock* being the operative word, he thought cynically... Marriage meant the end of his bachelor days.

He could not deal with Phoebe now. He needed time to think, and he had a breakfast meeting in an hour.

He walked around to where she sat, and laid a hand on her shoulder. He felt her jerk away from him, which angered him again.

'I have not time for this now,' he said curtly. 'I have meetings lined up all day that I can't miss, and I have to be in Greece by tomorrow evening for my father's birthday party.'

More important to Jed was the fact his father was retiring. The lawyers had been summoned, and tomorrow night he would be officially installed as the head of the Sabbides Corporation—the firm he had been running unofficially along with his own for the past few years. Not that Phoebe needed to know. His business had nothing to do with her.

'But don't worry—I will speak to Marcus before I go. He is an excellent doctor, and discreet. He will take care of your pregnancy, and I will pay for everything, I can assure you.'

She slowly lifted her head and stared at him for a long moment. She wasn't crying and her usually brilliant blue eyes were oddly blank.

'I'm not worried—and I'm sure he will,' she said quietly, and glanced back down at her clasped hands.

'Good.' Jed hesitated. He had never seen Phoebe look so subdued. Maybe he should say something. But he didn't do emotions, and he was still in shock, so he said, 'I need a shower,' and strode into the bathroom.

Ten minutes later, after a cool shower, he'd had time to think. Maybe he had been a bit harsh on Phoebe. Either by accident or design it didn't really matter—she was still a pregnant woman. He dressed swiftly and went looking for her. He found her sitting in the kitchen, with a cup of tea in one hand and stroking the cat curled up on her lap with the other. She loved the damn cat, which barely tolerated him, and for some reason that angered him further.

'I must leave now. I'll see you tonight and we can discuss the necessary arrangements.' Obviously he would set her up with an allowance straight away. As for the rest—once paternity was proved, everything could be organised.

Phoebe put the cup down on the table and glanced at Jed. He was immaculately dressed in a charcoal-grey suit, perfectly tailored to fit his broad-shouldered, long and lean

frame, and a white shirt and silk tie. How had she ever
imagined he was her boyfriend? she thought, appalled at
her own naivety. He'd reached thirty last month, and she
had splashed out and bought him a nineteenth-century solid
gold seal in the shape of a heart. She had spotted it in an
antiques shop, and thought he would see the symbolism in
her gift—that she was giving him her heart. How dumb was
that? He had never looked past her body, and now he had
decided it—she—had betrayed him. He was every inch the
successful tycoon, and she had been living in cloud cuckoo
land to believe otherwise.

She nodded her head, incapable of speaking to the ruthless, arrogant pig… He had ripped her heart to shreds with
his brutally cynical reaction to her pregnancy, cold-blood-
edly accusing her of being the worst kind of gold-digger,
plotting and planning to get pregnant and get his money.
That Jed—the man she loved—could actually think so
badly of her told her he had never really known her at all.
While she'd thought she had touched his heart, all she
had ever been to him was a willing female in his bed. His
mistress…

When he had casually told her his good friend the
doctor would discreetly 'take care' of her pregnancy—as
though her unborn child was less than nothing, a blip to
be dispensed with in the smooth running of his life—she'd
known it was over. Utterly finished.

Jed didn't want a baby. It was not on his agenda… What
kind of cold-hearted man was he that he could even equate
a baby with a business agenda? But then business was his
life and everything else was peripheral, she realised. A
termination was what he was offering her—not the love
and the support she had so stupidly expected. His solution
was to pay his doctor friend to make the baby go away.
Work, money, and the power that went with it were his

obsession, and she had been the biggest idiot in the world to think anything different.

Phoebe heard the door shut. Getting to her feet, she walked into the bedroom and fell flat on the bed. With her head buried in the pillow she finally let the tears fall. She cried with pain and grief for a love that never was, and the loss of her innocent illusions, and finally cried herself into a sleep of physical and mental exhaustion.

Phoebe awoke with a start and for a moment was completely disorientated. She glanced at the bedside clock. Three in the afternoon? What was she doing in bed? Then it all came flooding back...

Weakly she lay on the bed, going over and over again in her head every minute since Jed had arrived last night...the passionate lovemaking she had thought confirmed he loved her... Now she realised that to a sophisticated, highly-sexed man like Jed all she had ever been to him was little better than a sex slave, willing to do whatever he asked of her. The past year filtered slowly though her mind, and she was haunted by her own stupidity. All the gifts he had given her were nothing more than payment for services rendered in Jed's mind.

This morning, when she told him she was pregnant, the real Jed Sabbides—the poker-faced ruthless tycoon—had been revealed to her, and Phoebe shuddered in despair.

Jed's brutal reaction to her pregnancy appalled her all over again, and suddenly his parting words that he would discuss the necessary arrangements with her tonight replayed in her mind. She panicked.

She did not dare stay. Jed was a powerful personality, and deep down she did not trust herself to defy his obvious intention that she have a termination—because, heaven help her, she could not easily dismiss the love she felt for him, even knowing he was a complete bastard…

She had to leave Jed and the apartment—she had to pack. That was the only thought in her head as she leapt off the bed, heading for the chest of drawers and stumbling over the cat…

Jed Sabbides signed off on his conference call to the other side of the Atlantic. The two o'clock meeting he should have had in New York had been a success—another great financial deal brokered. It was seven-thirty in the evening, and he was finished work for the day. He ran a distracted hand through his thick black hair. He had with difficulty blocked all thought of Phoebe and her astounding news from his mind while working, but now he had no excuse.

He looked up as the door opened and Christina, his PA, walked in. 'Do you need me for anything else?'

'No,' he replied shortly. 'Go now.'

'You look tired, Jed. Let me get you a glass of whisky, and I'll give you a neck massage, if you like—it will help you relax.'

'The whisky, yes—the massage, no.' He looked at his PA, surprised she had suggested a massage. He must look worse than he felt, because it wasn't like her at all. Christina was dark-haired, not unattractive, and super-efficient. He was lucky to have her. There was no fear of Christina getting pregnant by mistake…she *never* made mistakes. But had Phoebe? he pondered. She was a lot younger, and he was her first lover. Maybe her pregnancy *was* a genuine accident.

'Here is your drink.' Christina placed the glass on his desk, with the bottle beside it, and moved to stand behind him. 'Are you sure I can't ease these tense muscles?' And suddenly her hands were on his neck.

'No.' He shrugged his shoulders, dislodging her hands. 'You leave, Christina, I am fine.'

'Okay.' She straightened, but not before—to his surprise—she bent her head to murmur against his ear. 'Don't forget we are flying to Greece tomorrow. Try to rest.'

Simple concern, he thought as the door shut behind her, and it reminded him how little concern he had shown for Phoebe's feelings this morning.

He picked up the glass of whisky and took a healthy swallow. He felt the warmth of the spirit flow down his throat. When had he become such a hard-nosed, cynical devil? he asked himself.

The shock he had felt at learning Phoebe was pregnant and he was about to become a father had worn off, and he was able to think clearly. He had never wanted to marry, but if he was honest he knew at some point in the future he would like a child—an heir to his fortune. He had had a happy childhood, with loving parents and his sister. The strain between him and his father had grown not just over business but over his multiple marriages following the death of Jed's American mother when he was seventeen. The most recent—number three since his mother—was thirty-five years his father's junior, and made a play for Jed whenever he went home.

Jed drained the glass of whisky and refilled it from the bottle, and took a swallow. He didn't trust women, with the exception of his mother and sister, and had never considered marriage. But he knew there was no way he would allow any child of his to be born illegitimate.

Phoebe—the beautiful, sexy Phoebe... Would it be such a hardship being married to her? he asked himself. He was her first lover, and the thought of her with any other man was not one he liked to contemplate. He took another sip of whisky.

Personally, he didn't believe in love—but he was Greek, and he did believe in the continuation of the family name. If he had to take a wife Phoebe was a good candidate. There was no denying the chemistry between them was fantastic—he had never had such great sex in his life— and he certainly wasn't keen to give her up. They had been together for over a year, which boded well for the future, and now she was pregnant with his child.

Jed drained his glass, picked up the phone and ordered the limousine he used when he did not want to drive. He got to his feet, his decision made. He would marry her. Surprisingly, he did not feel as trapped as he had first thought.

He glanced at his watch. Eight in the evening. He flicked on his cellphone to call Marcus and arranged to meet him for dinner. He was the one person he could discuss the situation with honestly, and he trusted him. What Jed knew about pregnancy could be written on a pinhead, and though deep down he didn't believe Phoebe had been unfaithful to him it made sense to check with Marcus when it would be possible to ascertain the fatherhood of a baby. It would do no harm for Phoebe to wait awhile for the wedding.

Leaving the room, he locked the door and took the lift to the ground floor. He said goodnight to the doorman and left the building feeling good.

He would tell Phoebe what he had decided, he thought magnanimously, and he could imagine the look of delight in her expressive blue eyes when she realised he was pre- pared to make an honest woman of her.

His arrogant confidence lasted over a leisurely meal with Marcus, during which he sought his friend's advice on Phoebe's pregnancy and told him his intention to marry her.

When they left the restaurant he told the driver to drop

Marcus off first. But his confidence took a hell of a knock when he finally got to her apartment—to find it empty except for the cat and an official-looking note on the hall table.

Phoebe lay flat on her back on the anonymous hospital bed, and stared sightlessly up at the white ceiling. She had cried for hours until she could cry no more, and now all she felt was numb and empty inside. She was oblivious to the noise and bustle which was typical of a Friday night in this London hospital, according to the elderly Dr Norman, the doctor who had treated her. Which London hospital she had no idea, and didn't care…

All she could hear was the doctor's voice as he told her she had lost her baby, but not to worry, apparently thousands of women miscarried in the first trimester—it was nature's way of dealing with a probably unviable pregnancy. But she was young, fit and could have more babies—no problem.

She knew he had been trying to be kind, trying to reassure her, but nothing and no one could ever do that. She put her hand on her flat stomach. She had only known definitely that she was pregnant for ten days, but the instant love and the need to protect her precious baby had been all-consuming.

Well, no more. Her baby was gone, and with the baby had gone her trusting foolish heart. Her life had changed irrevocably, because whatever happened in the future never as long as she lived would she ever forget the horror, the pain and the despair of this day.

The doctor had told her he would keep her in overnight and make an appointment for her to come back next week to have a D&C—dilation and curettage. Or as he'd explained, in layman's terms have her womb scraped. And then he'd told her to try and rest.

'Phoebe.'

She recognised Jed's voice and slowly turned her head. He was standing in the doorway, his immaculate suit not quite so immaculate, his jacket hanging open, with a look of shock and disgust in his dark eyes as he stared at her. She wasn't surprised. She wondered why she had never noticed until today how cold and ruthless he could be.

'I spoke to the doctor on my way in. He told me what happened. I am so sorry, Phoebe. But trust me you are going to be fine—I will make sure of it,' he said adamantly, casting a derisory glance around the room.

He was once more his cool, controlled self, Phoebe noticed. As for his 'sorry,' it didn't ring true, but she had not the will to care. Listlessly her eyes drifted up to the clock on the wall above his head, registering it was eleven-thirty.

'I can't believe the ambulance brought you here and you left me a note to feed the damn cat. You should have rung me or Dr Marcus. I've called him and sent a car to pick him up. He will be arriving any minute and we will get you out of this chaotic place.'

At the mention of Dr Marcus Phoebe closed her eyes. If it hadn't been for the thought of Jed hiring him she would not have panicked and she would not be here, she thought, reliving again the stab of pain that had made her clutch her stomach as she fell. Slowly, tentatively, she had straightened up and decided to make a cup of tea to try and ease the sharp ache, not wanting to take painkillers because of the baby. Then, sitting at the kitchen table, she'd realised something was really wrong. She'd dropped the cup and doubled over in a pain so severe it had stopped her breath. She'd felt the sudden flow of moisture between her thighs and stumbled to her feet as blood oozed down her legs. She'd grasped the phone and dialled the emergency number, but by the time the ambulance had arrived she'd feared it was already too late.

Six hours she had been here, and in that time the tiny life inside her had been expelled. She opened her eyes and looked at Jed again. The father of her baby. She realised his sensitivity was truly nonexistent. And as for trusting him—never again...

He actually had the colossal arrogance to suggest she should have called him. What a joke. It was heading for midnight now—he had obviously been in no hurry to get here. The numbness she had felt was replaced with the bitterly sad realisation that neither she nor her baby was as important to Jed as his latest business deal.

'No,' she said, and with black humour she almost smiled as the cosmic irony of the situation hit her.

Dr Marcus the terminator was no longer needed. Her panic, the cat and a corner of the chest of drawers had done the job for Jed. The knowledge gave her the strength to answer him back.

'It is not a chaotic place, but a very busy state hospital— the type we lesser mortals frequent. As for my moving, there is no point. I have already lost the baby. You should be happy now the problem is solved.'

For a long moment Jed Sabbides was struck dumb as the import of her words sank in. 'My God,' he groaned.

It was because of him that Phoebe was lying like a waxen doll in a hospital bed, and the guilt that had clawed at his gut from the moment the doctor told him more than he'd wanted to hear increased tenfold.

'Phoebe.' He crossed to the bed. 'I could never think of any child as a problem, and I am so sorry you lost the baby—you have to believe me.' Her beautiful face was as white as the sheet tucked up to her shoulders, her only colour the purple shadows under her red-rimmed eyes, and she looked hopelessly young.

Jed was stunned by the sorrow and the regret he felt when he looked down into her big blue eyes, no longer sparkling but dulled with the acceptance of what had happened to her. He felt like an ogre.

He was not an emotional man, but as he sat down on the edge of the bed he leant over and brushed his lips gently against her brow. He was appalled at the chill of her skin. He reached for her hand and she let him.

'You must believe me, Phoebe,' he repeated. Her hand was cold, and the look she gave him was equally cool. 'It never entered my head you might lose the baby. I was angry this morning, but by this afternoon I had got over the shock and decided I quite liked the idea of us becoming a family. I was going to tell you tonight.'

Easy enough for him to say that now, Phoebe thought, and felt the pressure of his hand squeezing hers. She looked up into his handsome face and for an instant imagined she saw pain and anguish in the depths of his dark eyes. Incredibly, she felt compassion stirring in her heart.

No, it wasn't possible. Jed was never going to make a fool of her again. His decision that he *quite* liked the idea of becoming a family was weak at best, and convenient for him, she noted. And tellingly, as the silence lengthened between them, he was in no hurry to expand on the subject, she thought, with a cynicism she had not known she possessed.

'Nice thought, but not necessary. My baby has gone,' she murmured. 'But look on the bright side, Jed. I have saved you a shed-load of money.'

'What do you mean by that?' Jed demanded, battling to contain the flash of anger he felt, knowing that in her fragile state the last thing Phoebe needed was him ranting at her. He had done enough of that this morning, and was filled with self-disgust at the memory. 'You can accuse me of a lot of things, Phoebe, but meanness is not one of them. Whatever you want you can have, I swear.'

The only thing she wanted was her baby back, and she could not have that. As for being mean, Jed was not mean but incredibly generous with material things, Phoebe recognised sadly. But with his thoughts, his emotions, he was the meanest man she had ever met—that was if he *had* any emotions, which she doubted. His self-control and his arrogant confidence in everything he did was incredible and he would never change. Jed Sabbides was always right…

'Yes, you are right,' Phoebe agreed. But with a faint spark of her former self surfacing she could not help adding, 'In the scheme of things the cost of a private doctor is nothing to you, I know.'

Jed had the niggling sense he was missing something, but Marcus had walked in with Dr Norman and a nurse, and, leaping to his feet, he demanded of his friend, 'I want Phoebe out of here, Marcus, and under your care immediately.'

'It's after midnight, Jed, and Phoebe is exhausted. Better to wait until the morning,' Marcus replied and Dr Norman agreed with him.

Jed wasn't satisfied. 'Marcus, I want the best for Phoebe, and this is not it.'

'I am not going anywhere,' Phoebe murmured, and all three turned to look at her. 'I just want to sleep.'

'She is right, gentlemen,' Dr Norman spoke up again. 'Let the nurse give her a sedative, and we can take this discussion outside.'

Phoebe stood in the kitchen, talking to the cat. 'You were right about the man, Marty. I should have trusted your instincts instead of mine. Jed Sabbides, for all his wealth, is emotionally and morally bankrupt—an utterly ruthless and despicable man, and I hate him.' The cat purred as if in agreement. 'But you belong to me now, and you and I are leaving.'

She picked up the cat and placed her in the pet carrier, then picked up the bag with the jewellery box inside and without a backward glance left the apartment. Her cases were already in the foyer and her car was parked outside.

Phoebe thanked the doorman for loading her cases, and after placing the pet carrier in the back seat of her car she fastened the seat belt around the box, slid behind the wheel and drove off.

When she had woken the morning after her miscarriage Jed had been there and Dr Norman had discharged her. Still devastated by her loss, she hadn't cared what happened to her, and when Jed had insisted he would take care of her she'd been too weak to resist, so she'd let him, and returned to the apartment.

Dr Marcus had provided a nurse to stay with her over the weekend, although Jed had insisted he could look after her. An appointment had been made at Marcus's private clinic for the D&C the following week, and after a lot of persuading from the nurse and Phoebe that he was fussing over her too much Jed had left that afternoon to attend his father's birthday party in Greece.

He had said, 'You have my mobile number—ring me if you need me. But I will be back on Sunday evening. You can count on it.' Then he had promised to take her to her appointment at the clinic the next week, kissed her good-bye, and left.

Well, it was now Monday, and the nurse had gone but Jed had not returned. After Phoebe had tried to to get in touch with him late last night a woman had answered his phone—Christina, his PA, apparently—and after an enlightening conversation Phoebe had known she was going nowhere except home…

She couldn't believe she had been so weak, so spineless, that she had let Jed fool her a second time—well, never again, she vowed…

The warmth and the love she had thought she felt for him had turned into cold, bitter contempt, and so she had done what he expected of a mistress. Taken everything he had ever given her, including the car.

It was little enough for the price of a child.

CHAPTER THREE

'I WISH you had told me it was the *Greek* Embassy, instead of just saying a foreign embassy,' Phoebe said, nervously chewing on her bottom lip. She certainly hadn't gone out of her way to put herself in the path of any Greeks in the last five years.

'What difference does it make? Foreign, Greek, French—the same crowd attends all of them. Stop worrying, Phoebe. You look stunning in that silver thing, and you fit in perfectly among the international elite of our capital city—in fact you are the best-looking woman here by a mile.'

'Flatterer, Julian! And my dress is not silver, but pale grey,' she informed her partner with a smile as they moved slowly in the line to be presented to the Greek ambassador to London. 'And this is a big step up for a history teacher from Dorset—an ambassador's ball.' And she would bet the simple jersey silk halter dress she was wearing was a fraction of the cost of every other woman's gown in the place.

'Rubbish! You studied politics as well as history, and you are smarter than most of the females here. Are you sure you wouldn't like to switch careers and join the Foreign Office in London with me?'

'No—and anyway, you are hardly ever in London, but

off all over the world on government jaunts most of the time.'

Julian shook his head. 'You know me too well, that is the trouble,' he said with a mock sigh.

Phoebe laughed, but it was true. He was three years older than her and he had known her almost all her life. Her Aunt Jemma had worked as his father's secretary for years, and after the old man's death Julian had inherited everything. But instead of taking over the full time running of the vast Gladstone estate, as his father had, he had hired an estate manager as he much preferred his government career.

Her Aunt Jemma lived in a cottage on the outskirts of a village on the estate, and Phoebe had spent part of the summer holiday at her aunt's for as long as she could remember. After her parents had died it had become her permanent home. Still was, she thought with a wry smile.

'Stop daydreaming, girl,' Julian quipped, 'It is our turn.' He stopped. 'Phoebe, meet Alessandro, our Greek ambassador and a good friend of mine—who, I might add, is a widower, and will be sorely missed by the ladies in the drawing rooms of London when he returns to his own country next month.'

Phoebe smiled at Julian's informal introduction and held out her hand to the distinguished-looking man standing in front of her. 'Pleased to meet you. I am Phoebe Brown.'

He was a very attractive man, with silver hair and a warm smile, and this ball was apparently his way of saying goodbye to the other ambassadors of the international community in London. Something Julian had omitted to tell her when he had talked her into attending the ball with him.

'The pleasure is mine, Phoebe. Now I understand why Julian has spent so much time in Dorset lately. It is always a delight to meet a beautiful woman.' His dark eyes twinkled, and she was flattered as he asked her a few questions about her life.

Beginning to relax, she held Julian's arm as he let her down the staircase into the elegant ballroom. He took a couple of glasses of champagne from a circling waiter and handed her one.

'Not as bad as you feared?' He touched his glass to hers. 'To an interesting night.'

Phoebe smiled and took a sip of the excellent champagne. 'You know, Julian, for once you may be right.'

The band struck up a waltz, and Julian took her glass from her hand and placed both on a nearby table. 'I'm sure I can do this,' he declared, wrapping an arm around her waist and taking her hand in his. 'I watched some celebrity ballroom dancing show while I was consigned to the country for so long.'

Phoebe laughed out loud. 'A few weeks with your legs in plaster and being convalescent for another two months watching television does not a dancer make,' she quipped.

'Oh, ye of little faith,' he mocked, and led her onto the dance floor.

Surprisingly, he was an excellent dancer, and Phoebe knew he had not really learnt from the television—though it was a fact that his enforced sojourn at the family manor in Dorset was the longest period he had stayed there in his adult life, after smashing both his legs in a motorcycle accident.

Julian, six-feet-two, twenty-nine years old, unmarried and undeniably handsome, with blond hair, grey eyes and a wicked smile, enjoyed playing the typical man about town. But after being a long-time family friend over the last few months he had developed his relationship with Phoebe into something a bit more. At first she had thought it was because, devoid of much female company in rural Dorset, he considered her his best bet. But his kisses were persuasive, and he had almost convinced her otherwise. Tonight they were staying at his London apartment after the ball, and though he had never said she got the impression he was hoping for a lot more than kisses. But, having been burnt before, she was still a bit wary.

In fact she wasn't sure she wouldn't have changed her mind if she had known the ball was at the Greek Embassy before they had arrived. But it was too late. Besides, no doubt her fears were groundless, she decided, and she *was* thoroughly enjoying herself.

'Penny for your thoughts?'

Phoebe grinned up at him. 'Oh, they are worth a lot more than that. If you are good, I will tell you later,' she teased, and he stopped for a second and held her closer.

'Trust me, I can be very good when the occasion arises.' The look in his eyes was sexually explicit.

'Behave yourself and dance,' she said, smiling, pleased by the sudden slight tingle of awareness she felt. Maybe tonight would be the right time to move on. She had certainly been celibate far too long...

Then the hairs on the back of her neck began to prickle, and she had the oddest feeling it had nothing to do with Julian. Someone was watching her.

Ten minutes later, standing at the bar in an adjoining room, Julian ordered a whisky and soda. He wasn't a champagne man. He ordered a fruit juice for Phoebe. One glass of champagne was enough for Phoebe, and she was thirsty. The barman served them and, picking up her glass, she took a refreshing drink before placing the glass back on the bar.

'This *is* an embassy, right?' she said, grinning up at Julian. 'So where is the Ferrero Rocher?' she teased. She was laughing with him when the ambassador appeared beside them and cut in.

'That advert is a very old joke,' he chuckled. 'But I am glad to see you two are enjoying yourselves. Now, allow me to introduce my daughter, Sophia.'

Phoebe turned slightly, her eyes still lit with humour, and shook hands with a smiling, raven-haired and very attractive woman.

'And this is her boyfriend, Jed Sabbides—chairman of the Sabbides Corporation.' The ambassador moved to one side. 'Our families have been friends for years,' he inserted, his voice filled with pride as he made the introduction.

At the mention of a name she'd hoped never to hear again Phoebe froze, and then he was standing in front of her, and she knew exactly who had been watching her. Her worst fear was stupefying reality.

Speechless and rigid with shock, she stared at him, and for a moment all she could see was the powerfully drawn face of Jed Sabbides, the man who had been her first lover. Her heart hammered in her chest and she drew in a deep, unsteady breath, willing the shock to recede.

He was wearing an elegantly tailored black dinner suit, as were all the men present, with a brilliant white shirt and black bow tie, and his eyes were equally black as they briefly met hers. He looked older, and there were a few threads of grey in the thick curly hair. The planes of his arrogant masculine face were a little sharper, and the lines around his eyes and bracketing his nose a shade deeper. He was in his mid-thirties now, and the extra years had only served to give him an even more impregnable self-assurance, but she would have recognised that harshly handsome face anywhere.

Only by a stupendous effort of will did she force her smile to stay in place as the introductions were made.

Would Jed admit he knew her? That was the question screaming in her mind. No, of course not—he was with his girlfriend, for heaven's sake.

'Phoebe.' A strong, long-fingered hand reached out for hers.

She steeled herself to take the hand he offered, 'Pleased to see you, Jed,' she said noncommittally, still not sure if he was going to admit they knew each other.

'The pleasure is all mine,' he offered, and the dark eyes that met hers were sardonically mocking. The brilliant charm of his smile that had so captivated her the first time they'd met had gone, lost in the hard tight line of his mouth.

She withdrew her fingers before he could clasp them, but even so she was horrified to feel a familiar electric spark at his brief touch, and glanced away, instinctively moving closer to Julian for protection.

Not that she needed any. Jed obviously did not think it necessary to acknowledge their former relationship, and as far as Phoebe was concerned that was a relief. Apart from Aunt Jemma no one in her life today—not even Julian— knew of her past connection with the man, and that was the way she wanted it to stay...

The conversation became general, and Phoebe threw in the occasional comment when Julian drew her into the conversation, but she studiously avoided looking at Jed Sabbides.

Her glance rested instead on Sophia, his girlfriend. She was petite and beautiful, and the gown she wore screamed haute couture—a red strapless number that had been designed to cling to her every curve. Sophia was just the type a Greek tycoon like Jed would finally settle for and probably marry, Phoebe thought cynically. Wealthy, with family connections, and of course Greek.

'Haven't I seen you somewhere before, Phoebe?' The deep accented voice slipped the question casually into the conversation, and she had no choice but to look at him again.

This time Phoebe didn't mind. Jed had never considered her good enough for him years ago—unlike Sophia, who apparently knew all his family and friends, Phoebe had been strictly mistress material. Now she realised she had had a lucky escape, because he certainly was not good for her now...

If he thought he could bait her with his sly questions he was wrong. Two could play at that game. She was no longer the naive girl he had seduced, but a mature women. Three years of teaching teenage girls more interested in boys than in learning had taught her to be assertive and resilient.

'No, you must be mistaking me for someone else. This is the nearest to Greece I have ever been.' *He* had certainly never taken her...

She saw the flicker of dark amusement in his eyes. The swine was enjoying this.

'Then maybe you are a model and I have seen your picture in a magazine?' he suggested, and she knew he was mocking her.

'No, I am afraid not.' Luckily for Phoebe his girlfriend took his arm, and stopped her from blurting out sarcastically that he had probably known so many women in his time the faces must blur together after a while...

'You men know nothing about modeling, Jed,' Sophia teased, hanging on to his arm. 'Phoebe is much too big to be a model. They are all reed-thin, coat hanger types.'

Phoebe stopped feeling slightly sorry for Sophia, having a ruthless, arrogant devil like Jed for a *boyfriend*. A misnomer if ever she had heard one. She decided they made a good match. Hidden behind the false smile and big brown eyes the woman was a bitch—with a huge bum, she thought rather cattily, not like her at all.

Phoebe *had* put on a couple of pounds in the past five years, though no one could call her fat. She taught physical education as well as history, and was well toned if slightly bigger in the chest. But there was a very good reason for that, and not one she wanted this pair to discover.

'Your girlfriend is so right.' She addressed Jed, but looked at Sophia. 'Actually, I teach history at a girls' school near my home,' she informed them. Then, picking up her glass from the bar, she took a sip of juice and wished she had never let Julian persuade her to come to the ball.

'History, Phoebe? An interesting subject. Which do you prefer to teach? Ancient or modern?' Jed asked, with a sardonic arch of a black brow.

The damn man was baiting her again, and she could not help it—she flashed him a fulminating look. 'Both.'

'Wise of you. Past history can teach us a lot about people,' he drawled.

Was she the only one who heard the cynicism in his tone? 'I'm pretty sure there is not much anyone could teach *you*,' Phoebe snapped, and stopped. Oh, hell! Why couldn't she have kept her big mouth shut? They were all looking at her as if she had taken leave of her senses. Maybe she had. Jed Sabbides had always had that effect on her. But she knew him for what he was and she hated the man.

Julian's hearty laugh broke the moment. 'Ah, Phoebe, I take back what I said about you joining the Foreign Office.' His arm came around her shoulders. 'You would never make a diplomat.' The three Greeks smiled rather condescendingly, Phoebe thought.

'You say what you think—a fatal flaw in a member of the diplomatic corps.' Julian dipped his head and brushed his lips lightly against hers. 'But in every other respect you are flawless, Phoebe,' he added.

For a brief moment Jed Sabbides was stunned by the sudden surge of anger he felt as Julian Gladstone kissed Phoebe. Five years since he had last seen her, since he had returned to find she had left him, taking everything he had given her and the cat...

He hadn't been pleased at the time, but after what had happened between them he hadn't been surprised and had moved on, taking it for granted she had done the same. Phoebe was nothing to him now, he told himself. But he could not resist teasing her, wondering how long she could keep up the lie about not knowing him.

Yet seeing another man actually kiss Phoebe had stirred a primitive proprietorial instinct in him he had thought long gone. And she was wearing diamonds *he* had gifted her, which somehow offended him even more—though she had certainly earned them. He had never had such a sexually compatible bed partner before or since Phoebe, and the realisation dented his firm control.

'I remember where I saw you, Phoebe.' Jed was no longer amused, but angered by her denial of him, and dropped all pretence. 'You were working as a receptionist in a hotel I stayed at once. You were a student at the time, I believe.' Let her wriggle her way out of that one.

'That's possible, I suppose,' she offered. 'I did once work part-time in a hotel, but a lot of people pass through a hotel reception and I don't remember all of them.' Implying he was not memorable...

The elegant woman now standing before him was the opposite of the innocent wanton Jed remembered. The silver-grey silk gown clung to her every curve, and the high heels she wore added to her above average height. She looked at him with cool blue eyes and, knowing he had been insulted, he reluctantly had to admire her defiant response. He did not remember Phoebe being so feisty in the past.

'Come on, Jed.' Sophia grabbed his arm. 'The band is playing our tune—let's dance.'

'Yes, of course,' he said, glancing down at Sophia, his anger abating and his control restored. He realised a trifle ironically that Phoebe enraged him but the woman he intended asking to marry him did the opposite—she left him cold.

He led Sophia on to the dance floor and held her close. The music was slow, her head was resting on his chest and he was content to leave her that way. It avoided his having to talk and gave him time to think.

He never usually attended this kind of gathering, but as Sophia had asked him and she was the ambassador's daughter he had agreed. They were staying at the embassy tonight, and he had decided it would be a good opportunity to do the conventional thing and ask her father for her hand in marriage before proposing.

Sophia was an attractive woman, well known for her voluntary work as a fundraiser for numerous charities in Athens. She was also a family friend and Greek, so she knew what was expected from a Greek wife, and if she was a bit stocky from the waist down he could live with that. She had good child-bearing hips—or so he had thought half an hour ago...

Sophia and her father had been opening the dancing, and he had stood at the top of the staircase, a glass of champagne in his hand. He had taken a sip and glanced idly around the room and stiffened, his dark eyes narrowing on the striking looking couple stopped in the middle of the dance floor.

The stem of the champagne glass had shattered in his

fingers. But Jed had dismissed the hovering waiter's concern, his eyes fixed on the couple. The man was tall and blond and the woman in his arms was Phoebe... There was no mistake. Her image was engraved in his mind for all time. Phoebe Brown...

Her fair hair was swept severely back from her face, revealing her exquisite features, her head was tilted back and she was smiling up at her companion. His intent gaze had followed the slender line of her throat down to the creamy curves of her breasts, the tantalising cleavage shown to advantage by the halter-style long dress she was wearing. He had shoved his hand into his pants pocket, surprised by the stirring of arousal he had felt looking at her. But then she had always had that affect on him, and seemingly nothing had changed...

He hadn't been able to take his eyes off her. Her partner spun her around and Jed had noted her once shoulder-length hair was much longer, and cascaded in gleaming waves down her back to end a few inches short of her narrow waist. Then he'd recognised something.

The diamond clip in the shape of a butterfly holding the sides of her hair at the crown of her head was a present he had given her. At the beginning of their affair he had teased her about shoving her hair behind her ears and fastening it with a rubber band. It was the first piece of jewellery he had bought her, and she had taken it with all the rest when she had left the apartment.

He had told himself at the time they were gifts, little enough for what she had gone through, and dismissed her from his mind. So why now was he bothered at seeing her wearing his gift when she was with another man? They were close—it was obvious by their body language. Almost certainly lovers, maybe even man and wife.

For some reason he did not question too deeply *why* he

wanted to know. Then he'd seen his soon-to-be fiancée and her father approach, and forced a smile to his lips. Feigning a mild interest in the tall blond man with a few judicious questions to the ambassador, he'd discovered a lot about him.

Apparently Julian Gladstone was a wealthy landowner, and a fast rising star in the Foreign Office, known for his brilliant linguistic skills. The ambassador knew little about Phoebe, but he'd offered to introduce Gladstone, saying Jed would like the man—everyone did...

Well, he had met him...and he didn't. Jed's lips formed a cynical twist. But he could see why Phoebe or any woman would... The younger man was the golden-haired Adonis-type, but the steel-grey eyes told him Gladstone was no push over. In other circumstances, he admitted wryly, he probably *would* have liked him!

'Jed, the band has stopped playing.' Sophia wriggled sensually against him and he felt nothing. 'You were miles away.' She pouted.

'Lost in your embrace,' he said smoothly, and with a hand at her back led her towards the group at the bar.

Sophia was not fooled, and in a sulk she made a beeline for Julian, fluttering her long lashes at him and suggesting they dance.

Jed's lips twisted again. Whether Sophia was a natural flirt or trying to make him jealous, he didn't care. Gladstone was too much of a gentleman to refuse her, and it gave Jed the opportunity to move in on Phoebe.

'That leaves you and me, Phoebe.' He saw the rejection in her brilliant blue eyes, followed by a stiffening of her spine and a determined tilt to her small chin. 'Dance with me,' he demanded, and wrapped his hand around her wrist before she could refuse him.

Phoebe had opened her mouth to say no, but the electric

touch of Jed's smooth palm against her skin made her catch her breath, and she was too late as his other hand slid around her waist and drew her against him and on to the dance floor.

The music was slow again…

She rested one hand on his broad shoulder, trying to keep some distance between them. Preferably the Arctic Ocean…

And why didn't this damn band play anything but mood music? she wondered as he moved her to the romantic rhythm with consummate ease. But her real problem was he was moving other parts of her she had considered thoroughly immune to him for years.

Get a grip…Jed Sabbides is just a man, like any other, and not a very nice one at that, she told herself. All she had to do was dance with him. She didn't have to speak to him. Turning her head slightly, she stared over his shoulder, but she could feel his dark eyes on her.

'Not looking at me won't make me go away, Phoebe.' He chuckled—a deep, throaty sound. 'So stop staring into space and tell me how you have been. Good, by the look of you. If anything, you are more beautiful than ever.'

She glanced up at him then. 'Thank you, I am fine,' she said, determined to be coolly polite. But it was difficult with Jed's arms around her and his piercing dark eyes holding hers.

'Then tell me why, given our past relationship, I get the feeling you wish you had never set eyes on me again. Even denying we had met?' he asked, with a mocking smile.

'Me?' Phoebe raised a delicately shaped eyebrow. 'I gave you the opportunity to acknowledge we knew each other when I said I was pleased to *see* you, instead of *meet* you. You didn't take it, and I understood why. Obviously you did not want to upset Sophia. But what I don't understand is why you started playing your stupid games. You should think yourself lucky I didn't blurt out the truth,' she said her blue eyes hard. 'Your fiancée does not need to know what a louse you are.' That knocked the smile off his face, she noted, and felt the sudden tension in his body.

'Sophia is not my fiancée.'

'Tell that to the ambassador, because I think he's hoping she is going to be very soon.'

'Sophia might have given him that impression,' he said, without any inflection whatsoever, 'but it is not necessarily true.'

'Well, for what it is worth I think you make the perfect couple.'

It suddenly occurred to Phoebe that if Jed was married and living in Greece with a family of his own she would feel a whole lot better and her secret would be safe.

'Now, why would you encourage me to marry? Maybe because you have plans of your own with regard to Julian Gladstone and you don't want me telling him about our affair and how it ended?' he mused. 'Is that it, Phoebe? You want to keep our tragic little secret?'

Her face paled. That he should remind her of the miscarriage was bad enough, but if Jed ever knew the whole truth...

'Don't be ridiculous. Julian and I have been friends for years, and he knows everything about me. I just think you and Sophia look good together.'

'And lovers for how long?'

'That is none of your business,' Phoebe said tightly.

He said nothing, just held her eyes with one of his disconcertingly astute looks. Then, from holding her hand loosely in his, he suddenly linked his long lean fingers with hers and clasped them against his broad chest.

Phoebe knew she was in deep trouble.

She felt the warmth of his other hand flex at the back of her waist, and his long fingers trailed gently up her spine to find the smooth skin of her bare back beneath the heavy curtain of her hair. The blood seemed to heat in her veins, and long forgotten sensations flooded through her.

She did not want to feel like this. She did not want to feel anything with this man. She stiffened, every nerve stretched to breaking point, as she fought to stay in control. All she had to do was get through the rest of this dance, this one evening, and she would never see Jed again, she told herself.

'Enough about other people, Phoebe,' Jed drawled huskily, and dipped his dark head, bringing his mouth very close to her ear. 'And enjoy the dance. You always loved dancing with me in the past and nothing has changed. Relax—you know you want to.'

He was so close she could inhale his clean male scent, the subtle hint of expensive cologne that was achingly familiar. His hand at her back stroked down and urged her into even closer contact with him.

Phoebe looked up and caught the sensual glitter in his eyes. Shockingly, she felt the hard pressure of his erection against her thigh, and a shiver snaked down her spine, curled in her belly. For a terrifying second she was tempted.

'The chemistry between us is still there, Phoebe. I can feel you trembling,' he declared huskily.

The girl he had known would have blushed and then eagerly melted against him. But Phoebe wasn't that person any more. She had more courage and more self-respect than to succumb to an arrogant, over-sexed swine like Jed, and more importantly she had more than herself to protect...

The knowledge gave her strength, and she lowered her hand from his shoulder to shove against his chest. Tilting her head back, she looked straight up at him. 'Remember where you are and save it for your girlfriend. As for trembling—that was a shiver of revulsion. You disgust me, Jed,' she declared scathingly.

She was fierce, and the deliberately aimed blow to his ego was savage, but Jed Sabbides was a threat to the comfortable life she had made for herself, and she wanted to make absolutely sure he would never want to see or speak to her again.

He stopped. He looked down at her and she could sense the tension in his big body. His hands fell to his sides and she could see it in the dark eyes that surveyed her from head to toe. His mouth was tightly compressed, and she expected him to explode with anger. But he didn't.

'A bit of overkill there, Phoebe, but I get your point. The music has stopped—shall we join the others?' And, taking her arm, he curled his firmly chiselled lips in a sardonic smile. 'By the way, I am glad to see you still wear the clip I bought you. It looks even better with your hair so much longer.'

Phoebe had forgotten all about the damn clasp in her hair. It was the only piece of jewellery she had kept, and now she wished she had not. She blushed...

Jed knew enough about women to know Phoebe had lashed out at him not because she was disgusted but because she was scared by her own response. 'So you can still blush, Phoebe.' And, lifting her chin with his finger, he looked deep into her eyes. 'I'm glad you kept something I gave you, Phoebe, though we both know it was not what you really wanted, and for that I am truly sorry,' he said sincerely.

Her reaction astounded him. She gasped and twisted her head away, but not before he caught the flash of panic laced with fear in her eyes. He reached for her arm, but she shrugged him off and walked swiftly back to Julian without a word in response.

Phoebe's reaction intrigued him. In his own way he had been trying to be compassionate by alluding to their shared past and her tragic miscarriage, not throw her into a panic, and he had to wonder why.

Seated in the back seat of Julian's chauffeur-driven Bentley, Phoebe asked him how far it was to his apartment.

'We are not going to my apartment, Phoebe, you can relax. I've instructed Max to take us back to Dorset. Much as I fancy you, I don't want to be a stand in for another man. The journey will take an hour or so—plenty of time for you to tell me all about Jed Sabbides. You did know him, didn't you?' he asked softly.

'Yes, I met him when I was at university.' And she told Julian everything.

It was cathartic in way, and it put her reaction to Jed in perspective again.

'The man did not strike me as that shallow, but it his loss,' Julian said, and put an arm around her. 'Forget about the rat.'

And she almost did…

Especially when on arriving home Julian smilingly warned her, "I'm not giving up totally, Phoebe. I'll be away for a couple of weeks or so and I'll call when I get back.' Then he kissed her lightly on the lips and left.

CHAPTER FOUR

IN THE Athens head office of the Sabbides Corporation a brooding Jed lounged back in a black leather chair, his dark gaze fixed on the folder on the desk in front of him. Leo Takis, a friend and the head of a security firm he often used, had delivered it personally fifteen minutes ago, with the comment that according to his English operative Sid there was not much to get excited about. Jed had been staring at the damn thing ever since…

Did he really want to open it? He had a busy day ahead of him, and a host of more important things to attend too. But in the two weeks since the embassy ball in London the smooth flow of his life had been shot to hell—all because of Phoebe Brown.

He could not concentrate on work.

He had not proposed to Sophia. Quite the reverse. He had told her it was not going to work and returned to Greece the next morning. One of the reasons being that since meeting Phoebe at the party Jed had found it impossible to get her out of his head. Sophia and her father would probably never speak to him again.

The more he thought about the way Phoebe had behaved that night, the more he had a gut feeling he was missing something. He was a good poker player, though nowadays he only played the occasional private big money game with a few like-minded friends. And in poker parlance he was great at reading 'tells'—and something was telling him Phoebe was trying to bluff him...

Her coldness, the way she had continued with the pretence that she had never met him before, the sensual response she had tried so hard to deny when he held her in his arms, and the odd look of fear and panic he had seen in her eyes as the music ended and they left the dance floor...

She had avoided so much as glancing at him again for the rest of the night—he knew because he had been watching her—and it had set his astute mind to wondering why.

Well—that was his excuse for hiring Leo's discreet security agency...

But in reality seeing Phoebe again had aroused a host of memories he had thought successfully banished from his mind years ago—the foremost of which was being buried deep inside her hot, sleek body, with her fabulous legs locked around him.

Jed grimaced. He had pretty much been in a constant state of arousal ever since—except unfortunately after the ball, when he had followed Sophia into her bedroom and taken her in his arms, nothing had happened!

It had crossed his mind to persist, to fantasise about Phoebe... But in that moment the uncomfortable truth had hit him. He had lied to himself for years. He had never had better sex than he'd had with Phoebe—in fact for two years after their parting he hadn't had sex at all! As for the couple of women since, he could not truthfully say whether or not what he had shared with Phoebe had been in some way responsible for his lacklustre and short-lived relationships with them.

With brutal honesty he had known then that his sensible plan to marry Sophia was never going to work. She was a friend, and deserved better than a husband who had no passion for her. Hence the break-up...

Jed picked up the folder. Inside was the details of Phoebe Brown's life from the week she had left the London apartment. He had given Leo that date specifically, as he knew all too well what had happened before... He weighed the file in his hand, and it felt light.

Good sign or bad? He didn't know, but what he did know was that he needed Phoebe back in his bed, to sate himself in her body and get rid of this lingering fascination for her once and for all...

Slowly he opened the file and began to read.

Five minutes later, he barely glanced at the photo of mother and child at the back of the brief report before dropping the lot on the desk. Then, swivelling in his chair, he stared out through the glass wall of his office into the bright light of the October sun. His broad brow creased in a thunderous frown and his dark eyes narrowed against the natural glare and the blaze of anger burning inside him.

A month after graduating from university Phoebe Brown had been back home, living with her aunt in a small village in Dorset—where Jed had guessed she had gone when he'd found the apartment empty. It was no surprise. She had spent a further year qualifying as a teacher, and was now employed in that capacity at a private girls' school in Dorset. She had bought a rundown cottage attached to her aunt's, and between them they had converted the property into one detached cottage. There she led a quiet, uneventful life with her family and was a well-respected member of the community and liked by everyone who knew her.

But what was a surprise, and what had caused Jed's unexpected flash of rage, was in the detail of that family...

Phoebe was a single mother of a boy of four years old. Not unusual in this day and age. But what he had instantly

realized, and what was anathema to Jed, was that the baby
had been born only seven months and one week after the
miscarriage of their child, and there was no father listed
on the registration of its birth.

He couldn't believe it. Deep down he didn't want to,
but he had too. It was there on the copy of the birth cer-
tificate. The baby had been born at Bowesmartin Cottage
Hospital in the county of Dorset. The baby must have been
premature—that was the obvious conclusion.

Well, the *sweet, innocent* Phoebe he had thought he
had known was nothing to him. She was the past, and
he should have left it at that. For all her beauty, she was
beneath contempt in his eyes.

For years he had carried a lingering sense of guilt over
what had happened between them, but not any more... So
much for her constant avowals of love. It simply reinforced
what Jed had always believed: there was no such thing as
love, and women always had an agenda...

Phoebe could not have taken more than a week before
falling into bed with another man and getting pregnant
again. Maybe she was type of women who wanted a child
more than she wanted a man? But in his experience it was
older career woman who fell into that category—biological
clock ticking syndrome, which certainly had not applied
to Phoebe at the time.

What did he care? His brief flight of fancy in consider-
ing resuming their affair was just that...a momentary blip
in his razor-sharp brain. Their relationship had finished
long ago. What Phoebe Brown did with her life was nothing to him...

Turning back to his desk, determined to dismiss her
from his thoughts once and for all and get some work done,
he reached for the folder to put it away and hesitated.

Something about Phoebe and her son did not add up…
With his vast experience in business and finance he knew
that after analysing all known facts and the people involved
if the figures were too incredible to be believed they were
invariably false.

He picked up the photograph and looked at it again more
closely. It had obviously been taken from a distance—
not that surprising, as taking unauthorised pictures of
young school children was a risky business in this day
and age—and there were other women and children in the
background. The features of the mother and child in the
foreground were clear enough, though the color of the eyes
was indecipherable, but it was definitely Phoebe standing
by the school gates, smiling down at the small, sturdy dark-
haired child holding her hand.

As he studied the image on the paper he had a sense of
recognition that built and built the longer he examined the
photograph.

He got to his feet, a steely and pitiless light gleaming
in his dark eyes. If his suspicions were correct, Phoebe
Brown had to be the greatest actress and the most devious,
contemptible woman he had ever had the misfortune to
meet.

With a face like thunder he walked into his secretary's
office and told her to cancel all his appointments in Athens
until further notice. He was going to visit the London office.
She must order the company jet to take him to England as
soon as possible. He didn't need Leo's agency for what he
had in mind. He was going to conduct his own very personal investigation, and if what he suspected was true he
vowed he would make Phoebe pay every minute of every
day for the rest of her life for her despicable lie…

* * *

'Has he been any trouble?' Phoebe asked her friend Kay, tightening her grip on Ben's hand as he tried to pull her down the drive to the village street.

'No, he was great. He played with Emma as good as gold.'

Phoebe lived on the outskirts of the village of Martinstead, and taught at a private girls' school in the nearby town of Bowesmartin. Kay, her friend and house-mate from student days, had visited her when Ben was born and ended up married to the local vet. Her daughter was eighteen months younger than Ben, and Kay picked him up from the village infant school where Emma was attending the nursery section and kept him until Phoebe got back about an hour later and collected him.

'Thanks. You have no idea how much I appreciate your taking care of him. Next week is half term, thank good-ness. So it will only be another six weeks after that before Aunt Jemma returns from her holiday—if that is okay with you?'

'Stop worrying, Phoebe. It's not a problem. Now go, it is cold out here.'

'Okay.' Phoebe laughed, and with a wave strolled down the drive to the pavement, Ben skipping along at her side.

Her aunt had gone on holiday to Australia, and in the four days since she'd left Phoebe had come to realise just how much she had depended on her aunt to help with Ben over the years. She had been there for Phoebe when she gave birth, and later looked after Benjamin while Phoebe qualified as a teacher and then worked.

When Ben had started school in September Phoebe had encouraged her aunt to finally take the two-month holiday she had been planning for ages, to visit her oldest friend in Australia. Her Aunt Jemma deserved the break. She had always loved Phoebe and been there for her, and in the last few years for Ben as well, of course.

Phoebe glanced down at her son. He was lucky and so was she.

Being a teacher was an advantage for a single mum, she thought contentedly. She had the same holidays as the infant school, and next week she could relax with Ben. They were going to redecorate his bedroom. She had never got around to removing the baby blue décor, and Ben now wanted either racing car or dinosaur-printed wallpaper, but he had not decided yet.

'Mum! Mum!' he yelled, and stopped, forcing her to stop as well.

'Yes, darling, what is it?' she asked.

'Can I have a car like that one over there on my wall?' He was pointing at a car parked on the opposite side street of the street.

She chuckled. It was a low-slung lethal-looking black monster, with huge wheels, illegally parked in front of the post office—just the sort to appeal to young boys or old, she thought dryly.

'Mum, Mum—can we go and see what kind of car it is…?'

But Phoebe barely heard Ben's excited request as the car door opened and a man stepped out.

Long and lean, he wore black hip-hugging jeans and a heavy black rollneck sweater, and he looked as dark and dangerous as the car…

Jed Sabbides…

She watched in stunned amazement as in a few lithe strides he was over the road and standing in front of her.

'Phoebe, this *is* a surprise. I thought it was you, but the child threw me when I heard him call you Mum.'

His deeply voiced greeting set every nerve in her body

on edge, and she could do nothing about the sudden leap in her pulse. Steeling herself to remain calm, she glanced up at him and politely said, 'Hello, Jed,' conscious of her son at her side.

'I wasn't aware you had a child. Nobody told me.' Jed's piercing black gaze sliced through her like a knife, and she had never seen such rage—quickly controlled as he turned his attention to her son.

'Hello, young man. I heard you telling your mum you liked my car.' He smiled down at Ben. 'It is the latest model Bentley convertible.'

'Wow! Does that mean the roof comes off?' Ben asked with eyes like saucers.

'Yes, at the press of a button. Would you like to see inside? Or I have a better idea—let's go for a drive.'

'No,' Phoebe snapped, tugging Ben closer to her side. 'He knows he must never get into a stranger's car.' And she wished he had not yelled 'Mum!' quite so loud—not that it would have made much difference.

Jed turned his head and stared down at her, and the look in his eyes made her blood freeze.

'Admirable. But you and I are not strangers, Phoebe, so there is no harm in introducing me to your son, is there?' he queried silkily.

He knew… That was her first thought, then common sense prevailed. Jed might have his suspicions, but he could not possibly know for certain—and she was not about to tell him.

She stood very still and moistened her suddenly dry lips with the tip of her tongue as she considered her options. She could walk off with Ben and ignore Jed, or to allay any suspicion he might have she could be polite. Good manners won.

'Ben,' she said, looking down into her son's upturned

face, 'this is Jed.' She swallowed hard, forcing a smile to her stiff lips. 'We used to know each other.' She would not lie and call the man a friend. 'Say hello.'

Ben looked at her with a hint of puzzlement in his eyes, then shifted his gaze to stare solemnly up at Jed. 'Hello, Jed. I am Benjamin Brown. I live at Peartree Cottage, Manor House Lane in Martinstead.'

Phoebe wanted to scream. Last year she had spent weeks teaching Ben to say his name and address, in case he ever got lost, and now he reeled it off to the last man she would ever want to know it.

Then her traitorous son looked back at her, a big grin on his face. 'So *now* can I have a ride in the man's car, Mum?'

She shook her head helplessly—her son was as sharp as a tack—and before she could answer Jed cut in.

'Yes, of course you can, Ben. I'll give you and your mum a lift home.'

How dared Jed presume to answer Ben for her? He had no right, and her maternal instincts were aroused along with her temper. She told him straight.

'No, you won't. Apart from anything else—' like deciding in his high-handed manner what they would do, she thought scathingly '—it is illegal for a child to travel in a car unless a child seat is fitted, and I doubt you have one or that this model is equipped to have one fitted.' She cast a disparaging glance at the black monster. 'We will walk home.'

'But, Mum—'

'Sorry, son. Your mother is right.'

Jed glanced at her, and she saw the cynical twist to his lips. Her heart sank to her boots at his casual use of the word *son*. She suspected it was not casual at all...

Somehow he knew. But how he had found out she had

no idea—and, given the one memorable occasion Jed had clearly told her he didn't want a child, saying having a child was not on his agenda, why he was getting involved surprised her...

'Yes, but there is a seat in Mum's car you can use if you come home with us. Can he, Mum?'

'What?' She stared at Ben, the bright, clever child she was so proud of, and wished just for once he was not so smart. He had an answer for everything and was usually right—just like his father, she thought despairingly, and heard Jed laugh.

'Good idea, Ben, if your mother will agree.'

Two sets of identical brown eyes fixed on her, anticipating her answer. The boy's pleading, the man's hard and mocking.

The last thing she needed was for Jed to know she still had the car he had given her—the hairclip at the ball had been enough of an embarrassment—and she wanted to say no. Instead she prevaricated.

'I don't think that is a good idea. It is quite difficult, taking the child seat in and out of my car. Plus it is getting late, and you have to have your tea—and remember, Ben, your bedtime is seven-thirty.' She listed every excuse she could think of. 'And I am sure Mr Sabbides is a very busy man. Maybe some other time.'

'Not so busy. But I take your point about the seat, Phoebe.' His tone mocked her. 'I have an idea.' Glancing at his watch, he smiled down at Ben. 'While you and your mum go home for tea I have a few calls to make. But I'll be back by six, with a car seat, and we can go for a spin then—how does that sound?'

Horrendous, Phoebe thought bitterly. But, seeing the beaming smile on her son's face as he asked her if that was okay, she hadn't the heart to disappoint him again.

'If Mr Sabbides is sure, that is fine with me,' she lied.
'I'm sure.'

He gave her a cold, hard glance, and she had the sinking sensation he was not just talking about a car ride. But
with a bit of luck, she thought, clutching at straws, even
Jed might not find it so easy to procure a car seat in the
rural depths of Dorset at four thirty on a Friday evening.
Weymouth on the coast was the nearest town with shops
that sold such things, and he might give up, or get lost...

The last would be her preference.

'I will be back, Phoebe. You can count on it.'

His voice was deep and menacing, and it made her want
to grab her son and run. But instead she met his dark eyes
with her own icy blue, her lips twisting in a bitter smile as
a memory of another time and place replayed in her mind.
'So you say.'

Jed had said the exact same words to her when he had
left to go to Greece for his father's birthday and he had lied
then. Remembering the past gave her the determination to
stand up to him. He had not wanted a child five years ago,
and he sure as hell was not getting hers now...

'Believe it,' he declared, and ruffling Ben's hair with
his hand added, 'See you at six, Ben.' He strode back to
his car and drove off.

Jed Sabbides clasped the wheel white-knuckled and ma-
noeuvred the car at a reckless speed through the narrow
country lanes towards Weymouth, his head spinning. He
hadn't been expecting to meet them. He had merely stopped
at Martinstead post office to ask directions to Peartree
Cottage, and had just slid back behind the wheel of his car
when he'd caught sight of Phoebe walking down the drive
of the house opposite.

She was wearing a red wool jacket, a short black skirt,

black leggings and black ankle boots. With her pale hair knotted on top of her head and her face free of make-up she'd looked stunning and as sexy as hell. Then his attention had focused on the child holding her hand, and even though he had been half expecting it he had frozen in shock. The child at her side looked very like photos of himself at that age…

Ben was his. He would bet his life on it. But it made no sense…

A week ago, looking at the picture of mother and son, he had felt his suspicion aroused. The first thing he had done when he'd got to London was contact Marcus and arrange to have dinner with him the following night. Over a leisurely meal, after reminiscing about their student days, the past in general, Jed had quizzed him about the miscarriage without mentioning that Phoebe had had another baby. He didn't want to look like a paranoid idiot! Marcus had confirmed there could be no doubt Phoebe that lost her baby. He had consulted with Dr Norman at the time and read the medical notes. The sex of the child had been indistinct. Then, having drunk more than he should, Marcus had admonished Jed for leaving such a delightful young woman and had recalled that she had not kept her appointment at his clinic—not surprising, under the circumstances.

Jed had made no comment; there was no reason for Marcus to know it had been the other way round. His ego had taken enough of a battering where Phoebe was concerned. He'd seen his old friend safely home—and the next morning he had tried to double-check with Dr Norman— who unfortunately had died some time ago.

Was it possible the doctors had been wrong?

They had to have been! Somehow Phoebe had lied and fooled them all into believing she had miscarried. Because when he had approached her earlier he had seen the same look of fear and panic in her eyes he had noticed at the ball, when his suspicions she was hiding something had first been aroused.

Hiding his son from him… If he was right, she needed to be very afraid, and he vowed to make her suffer for every day of Ben's life he had missed.

While Ben happily played on the kitchen floor with his racing cars, Phoebe prepared their dinner, her thoughts in turmoil.

Jed suspected something. He had to. Because it could not possibly be a coincidence he was here. Martinstead was well off the beaten track, with a single road through the village that led only to Gladstone Manor. Residents and visitors had to drive in and out the same way. But who could have told him? Not Julian. She was sure he was far too discreet.

Carrying two plates of grilled sausages, mashed potatoes, peas and carrots across the kitchen, she put them on the scrubbed pine table and, turning, picked Ben up and gave him a big hug. She needed to hold him to reassure herself that Jed was no threat to their happy life.

'Your favourite sausages because I love you,' she told him, then let him wriggle out of her arms and onto the chair. Kissing the top of his head, she sat down on the chair opposite. She had never felt less like eating in years, but she managed a few mouthfuls—more for Ben's sake than hers. She had to set a good example.

Oh, God! What kind of example would a ruthless, cold-hearted man like Jed be to her son, with his fast cars and faster women?

In that moment her mind was made up. Jed had no proof Ben was his, and as long as she denied it there was precious little he could do about it. If he tried she would show him he could not intimidate her, and would fight him every step of the way...

Phoebe looked at the clock. Six-forty-five—Jed was late... She cleared the table and washed the dishes in between answering a constant flow of questions from Ben about Jed's car, and what the time was, and when the man was coming back. With a bit of luck Jed would never return. The heartless jerk had never returned when he'd promised *her* he would—why would his promise to her child be any different? Ben might be upset for a while, but he would get over his disappointment—problem solved.

'Right Ben.' She dropped down beside him on the floor in the sitting room. When it had reached half past six she had finally persuaded him to settle down and watch the children's channel on television. 'Bathtime, story and bed.'

'But what about my ride in the car? Your friend promised.'

The disappointment in his brown eyes touched her heart. He was so young and innocent, and she did not want to be the one to destroy his trust. 'He must have been delayed; maybe he will come another day.'

'Do you think so?'

'Oh, I am sure he will.' A wry smile curved her mouth as Ben leapt to his feet, his happiness restored—while hers was in danger of being destroyed with the arrival of Jed into her nice, well-ordered life.

'Okay, can I have the speedboat in the bath?' he asked—just as the doorbell rang.

Oh, hell! She swore under her breath, but Ben was already out of the sitting room and running to the front door.

Phoebe followed and opened the door. Jed was standing

on the doorstep, a broad smile on his face for Ben, who had pushed past her.

'You came back. Mummy said you would.'

'Your mummy knows me well. And I have got a child seat fitted, so if she agrees we can take that ride now.'

'You are late,' Phoebe snapped, angry because to her horror her heart had leapt at the sight of him and she realised she found Jed as incredibly attractive as ever. 'Ben's bedtime is seven-thirty.'

But she wasn't surprised Jed had managed to get a car seat. The man could find a lake in a desert if he wanted too. What did surprise her was that he had got a state-of-the-art child and booster seat combined, fitted in the *front* passenger seat. She wasn't sure it was allowed by law for a child to travel in the front seat, but when she tried to remonstrate with Jed he dismissed her concern, informing her the shop that had sold him the seat had assured him it was okay.

'Well, it had better be a quick trip,' she finally conceded.

Fifteen minutes later she was sitting stiffly in the back seat of the car, silently simmering with resentment. Jed had demonstrated as soon as they got in the car how the roof rolled back, much to Ben's delight. She supposed she should be grateful he had closed the damn thing. But all she felt was a growing sense of dread. There was no escaping the fact that Ben was happy and completely at ease with his new-found friend, and she wondered what evil trick of fate had landed her in this mess.

She could hear the excitement in Ben's voice as Jed gave him what sounded like instructions on how to drive over the roar of the engine. She wanted to yell at him that her son was only four, and tell him to slow down while she was at it. But she knew it would be futile. She had forgotten Jed's penchant for driving like a bat out of hell.

Glancing out of the window, she saw they were actually at Bowesmartin. It usually took her thirty minutes to get to the town, but Jed had covered the distance in half the time. She hoped he got a speeding ticket, and wished she had not told him to make the ride quick as Ben had to go to bed soon.

Hoist by her own petard, she thought wryly.

More than she could ever have imagined possible, she realised a minute later, when the car ground to a halt as the traffic lights outside Bowesmartin Cottage Hospital changed to red and she heard Ben chattering happily to Jed.

'That's where I went when I broke my arm, and the man said I was very brave when he mended it,' she heard Ben bragging cheerfully. 'Mum had me there, and I am a miracle baby—because I had a twin, but it died before I was born.'

Phoebe closed her eyes, the colour draining from her face. Why, oh, why had she taken the advice in the baby books so literally and told her son the truth? She must have been crazy—because now it had come back to bite her with a vengeance.

'That is very interesting, Ben,' she heard Jed respond.

She opened her eyes and saw he was watching her in the driving mirror.

'Out of the mouths of babes, Phoebe?' he mocked, and the gleam of bitter triumph in his eyes chilled her to the bone.

'I am not a baby. I am nearly five and a big boy now,' Ben stated, saving her from responding. Thankfully Jed's attention was diverted from her back to Ben.

Phoebe stared blindly out of the window as the lights

changed and Jed drove on. Ben *was* a miracle baby, and her mind drifted back to the past as the familiar landscape sped by.

She had been back living with Aunt Jemma for nearly two months when she had finally told her aunt about her disastrous love affair and the miscarriage she had suffered. The reason being that a week earlier she had visited her local GP because she had still been suffering from slight nausea and a bloated feeling, and she had been worried something was wrong. She had told her GP she had suffered a miscarriage seven weeks earlier, but she couldn't recall the name of the London hospital, only Dr Norman. She'd seen no point in mentioning Jed or Dr Marcus, though privately she had been worried she had been too hasty leaving London without having the D&C procedure.

Phoebe could still remember the sense of awe and wonderment after her GP had asked a few pertinent questions and then examined her and sounded her stomach as well as her chest. She had told her she was about sixteen weeks pregnant, and the baby was fine. He'd arranged for her to have an ultrasound scan at the local hospital and told her she had nothing to worry about. It was a rare occurrence, but originally she must have been carrying twins—not identical—and had lost only one.

CHAPTER FIVE

PHOEBE considered herself lucky that five years ago she had failed to keep her appointment with Dr Marcus for the D&C procedure after all... But she didn't feel lucky now as she walked out of Ben's bedroom and closed the door quietly behind her. He was fast asleep, her beloved innocent child, but she knew she would get no sleep tonight, with Jed's threat still ringing in her ears.

When they had arrived back at the cottage earlier Ben had thanked Jed for the ride in his car, then added, 'It *is* a super car, but I like the colour of Uncle Julian's better. His is bright red.'

Phoebe had had to smile at the look of masculine pique on Jed's handsome face.

'So, Ben, you like red and Uncle Julian, hmm?'

'Yes—he is my friend and Mum's, like you,' Ben had replied happily as they'd walked up the path to the door.

'I will remember that,' Jed had offered as he'd said good-bye to Ben.

Phoebe's smile had vanished when his dark head had bent towards her.

'Uncle Julian be damned! I will be back later, and you'd better have some answers ready,' he'd hissed with sibilant softness, before walking off.

Thinking about Jed's threat was doing her no good at all,

Phoebe decided as she entered her bedroom and removed her now damp clothes—bathing Ben was a lively operation at the best of times. She dressed in a pair of faded jeans and a blue shirt and, picking up a brush from the dresser, pulled out the few pins remaining in her once elegant topknot. She gave her a hair few vigorous strokes before flicking the long length behind her ears and fastening it with a simple band, then left the bedroom.

Quietly she descended the stairs and turned towards the kitchen at the back of the cottage. A soothing cup of tea that was what she needed. There was no point stressing over a knock on the door that might never happen, so she picked up the kettle, took it to the sink, filled it with water and switched it on. She opened one of the kitchen cupboards and took out a mug, a faint smile curving her mouth. It had been a present from Ben last Christmas, with the help of Aunt Jemma, and the inscription on the white porcelain proclaimed the owner to be the 'Best Mum in the World'.

A timely reminder! Her position was clear, and if Jed Sabbides turned up again all she had to do was remember she *was* a great mum and tell him to take a hike…

Phoebe carried the mug of tea into the sitting room and sank down on the long, large soft-cushioned sofa that curved into an open end, in a modern take on a chaise longue, and faced the fireplace. Her aunt had insisted on buying the sofa, saying she had spent sixty years with old-fashioned furniture and wanted something different. Actually, it worked quite well—though Ben spent a lot of time perched on the open end because it was closest to the television…

She took a sip of her tea and thought of lighting the log fire, but it wasn't worth it this late, she decided. Picking up the remote, she switched the television on, flicking through the channels, but there was nothing that captured her interest.

Sighing she glanced around the room. She loved this house—her home… It had originally been a nineteenth-century stone-built semi-detached farm labourer's cottage, two up and two down, belonging to her aunt. When the cottage next door had come on to the market four years ago, with the help of a diamond necklace and some other unwanted jewellery Phoebe had bought it.

With Aunt Jemma's agreement she had converted the two into one good-sized detached house. Consequently the entrance hall was surprisingly spacious, with a single new wide oak staircase. On one side was the sitting room, which stretched from front to back, and on the other side the original front room had been left to provide a dining room that doubled as a study. At the rear was a large L-shaped family kitchen, and upstairs there was a bathroom and three double bedrooms—her aunt's with an *en-suite* bathroom—a family bathroom, her own room, and the third bedroom over the hall: Ben's room… A gravel drive ran down one side of the house, and with a new garage built at the bottom of the garden the conversion was complete. And a great success Phoebe thought, glancing contentedly around.

A big armchair stood at one side of the fireplace, with a tall standard lamp behind it and a mahogany bureau against the wall. On the other side was the television. In the centre was a coffee table, and a Persian rug in shades of turquoise was spread in front of the fire, providing a nice contrast with the oak wood floor. Beneath the front window was an antique desk and chair of her aunt's, and beneath the back window an old sailor's trunk Phoebe had picked up at a car boot sale that was ideal for storing some of Ben's toys. Maybe not the height of fashion, but in the soft glow of the standard lamp it was warm and welcoming—a real family room.

Unfortunately she had a sinking feeling that her happy home might be about to change, if Jed had his way. Draining her mug of tea, she rose to her feet and headed back to the kitchen.

She was worrying for nothing, she told herself determinedly. Jed could not take her child unless she let him, and she was not that dumb. She rinsed out the mug and put it back in the cupboard, and with a last look around the kitchen decided to mark papers for a while.

Ensconced in the study over an hour later, she was chuckling over an essay Elizabeth Smith—one of her sixteen-year-old students—had written. According to her, the French Resistance fighters in World War II had used the internet to publicise their cause!

Then she heard the knock on the door. She toyed with the idea of not answering, but she didn't want Ben disturbed and reluctantly got to her feet. Moment of reckoning, she thought as she walked down the hall, rubbing her suddenly damp palms down her slender thighs. It could only be one man.

Taking a deep breath, she opened the door.

It was dark out, but the light from the hall illuminated the tall figure of Jed, his hand raised as if to knock again—but then patience had never been one of his virtues, she recalled. When he wanted something, be it a business deal or a woman, he went straight for his objective with all the skill and guile at his disposal. As far as she knew he had never failed. But there was always a first time, she told herself...

The dark eyes surveying her were inscrutable, but she sensed the tension in his broad shoulders. Phoebe straightened, keeping her spine rigid. He was wearing the same casual clothes, with the addition of a leather jacket, and now dark stubble shadowed his square jaw. If anything he looked more dangerous and more intimidating than before. Suddenly she was aware of how isolated the house was, situated at least a ten-minute walk from the village, and how alone she was with only a sleeping child for company. Her heart beat a little faster.

'It is rather late to be calling. Anything you wish to say to me can wait until the morning. I want an early night.' And, tightening her grip on the door handle, she began to close the door. But a strong hand closed like a vice around her wrist.

'Who with? Uncle Julian?' he drawled, his big body crowding her as he urged her back into the hall and closed the door behind him.

'Don't be disgusting—and I would like you to leave,' she continued doggedly, determined to remain polite but firm. She tried to ignore the sudden leap in her pulse beneath his enfolding hand, and made herself look steadily up at him.

Big mistake… His dark eyes burned like living coals of fire into hers, and she could not tear her gaze away.

'Why, damn you? Why?' he demanded, taking her hand behind her back to pull her close against his tall frame. 'You told me you were pregnant swiftly enough. What the hell did I do so wrong that a few months later you would deny me knowledge of my son?'

She saw the fury, the angry confusion in his eyes, and ignoring it flung back her head. 'He is not your son,' she declared defiantly. It was a desperate last-ditch attempt to get him to leave. She was aware of the tension in him, and also aware of the pressure of his hard body against her own. She had never known a man who could affect her physically as strongly as Jed did, and she trembled. He felt her telltale tremor, Phoebe knew, as his dark eyes narrowed with a more sinister light.

'I know you for the liar you are, and I could strangle you for what you have done to me and mine.' His free hand snaked around her neck, his long fingers grasping the thick swathe of her hair and twisting it around his wrist, pulling her head back. 'But don't worry. There are other ways to make you suffer.'

Held captive in his hold, she stared helplessly into his dark eyes and recognised the menacing sensuality in the darkening depths. 'No,' she choked, and splaying her hands defensively against his broad chest tried to break free. But he pushed her hand higher behind her back, forcing her harder against him as his dark head descended and he subdued her with a brutal kiss.

His hand at her nape held her head firm as he ravaged her mouth with a ruthless, domineering passion that Phoebe fought to resist. But, trapped against his broad chest, it was a useless exercise.

Indifference was her only hope, but it was a futile hope as the demanding pressure of his firmly chiselled lips against her own and the thrusting of his tongue into the moist interior of her mouth, the achingly familiar taste of him, incredibly awakened a long-denied desire. She tried to force the physical memories back, but her traitorous body had a will of its own and it betrayed her. Her breath caught in suffocating excitement as a curl of heat ignited in her belly, sending her pulse rate rocketing and making her shudder in involuntary response.

Sensing her reaction, he gentled his mouth and trailed his lips to the long, slender arch of her neck, closing over the wildly beating pulse in her throat. She was scarcely aware when his arm eased around her waist and the hand holding her hair slipped down to cup her breast through the soft fabric of her shirt.

His thumb rubbed lightly across her burgeoning nipple, and it was only when the hot stab of arousal arrowed from her breast to her groin, tightening her wayward flesh, that she realised the very real danger she was in—almost too late…

'Get your hands off me, you great brute.' She twisted, dislodging his hand from her breast and breaking free from his restraining arm, and fell back a step.

Jed stared at her for a long moment, his dark eyes hard, and then he laughed—a cruel sound in the fraught silence. 'You still want me, Phoebe. I felt your heart pounding, your body shaking,' he mocked

'With anger…' she said, fighting down the shameful desire that pulsed through her body. 'You repulse me,' she lied, stunned by the ease with which Jed had almost seduced her again.

'No, I don't,' he sneered. 'But I don't expect a deceitful little bitch like you to admit the truth.'

It was the cold, hard arrogance of his tone as much as the words that got to Phoebe, and without a second thought she swung at him, landing a hard slap on his handsome face as she yelled, 'Get out of my house now or I will call the police!'

'No.' He caught her hand and almost dragged her into her own living room. 'And keep your voice down—you will wake Ben.'

'I don't need you to tell me how to look after my son,' she said defiantly, but knew Jed was right. She was angry with herself almost as much as him, and she had let her temper get the better of her. But the damn man was always right… It was another character trait she hated about him, along with his superior attitude and his arrogance.

'Sit down.' He pressed her backwards and she felt the sofa at the back of her knees.

Though she was loath to admit it, she was grateful to sit down. Her legs felt weak, and she had not yet got over the power of his kiss, nor her unwelcome response to him.

'I forgive you the slap, because maybe I was a little harsh, but it was a choice between kissing you or wringing your beautiful neck. Lucky for you the former was my choice, but you should know by now there is nothing that more arouses a man's passion's than a challenging woman.'

'I don't believe you said that. A male chauvinist pig has nothing on you.' Phoebe shook her head. 'You belong in the Dark Ages.'

'No, I belong with my son.' He stared down at her, his expression cold. 'That is why I am here and why we have to talk.' He shrugged off his jacket and dropped it on the arm of the sofa before adding, 'But first I could use a drink.'

The sight of Jed in a body-hugging sweater that outlined his muscular chest in every detail was not something she dared contemplate for long and, tearing her gaze away, she got to her feet.

Anything to put off the conversation he was angling for, Phoebe decided, had to be good.

'Tea or coffee?' she asked.

'Have you anything stronger?'

'Only wine.' Not waiting for his response, she left the room, glad to escape his powerful presence for a few minutes and trying valiantly to get her thoughts into some kind of order.

Five minutes later she walked back into the living room with two glasses and a bottle of white wine in her hands.

Jed was standing by the bureau. He had picked up a silver-framed photograph of Ben and was studying it intently.

Out of nowhere her heart squeezed at the look of wonderment she saw in his eyes, and as she watched she saw him trace with one finger what she knew was the outline of Ben's smiling face.

'Wine,' she muttered, placing the glasses on the coffee table. 'Not the vintage you are used to, and the bottle has a screw top,' Phoebe said as she opened the wine. 'But then the experts are now saying a cork is not necessarily better.'

She was babbling, but seeing the awe and the tenderness on his face as he studied Ben's picture had unsettled her.

She didn't want to feel anything for Jed, and he certainly did not deserve her sympathy. Filling the two glasses, she sat back down on to the sofa. Reaching for a glass, she took a sip.

'How old was Ben here?' Jed held up the picture frame.

'Two.' She didn't want to talk about Ben with Jed. She didn't want the man anywhere near her son. But she had a horrible feeling she was not going to have much of a choice.

'And here as a baby, with Julian Gladstone and the other person? I presume it is your Aunt Jemma?'

'Yes, Julian is an old family friend, and as for Aunt Jemma, you never met her because you were always too busy, I seem to recall. The picture is Benjamin's baptism photograph—they are his two godparents.'

'Julian Gladstone is my son's godfather?' he queried, with such a look of outrage Phoebe almost smiled.

'He is *my* son's godfather,' she amended. 'And Julian is a very good one. His house is a mile up the road and they see a lot of each other. Ben really likes him.' Not so subtly she was letting Jed know Ben did not need a billionaire Greek flitting in and out of his life when he had an excellent male role model virtually on the doorstep.

Jed made no reply, and Phoebe watched warily as he carefully placed the picture back on the bureau and strode over to sit in the armchair by the fire. Reaching for his glass, he took a deep swallow. Only then did he look at her, his scornful gaze skimming over her mutinous face.

'Give it up, Phoebe. We have established Ben is mine— he virtually told me so himself in the car,' he drawled sardonically. 'I am not a fool, and your pathetic attempt to needle me over Julian Gladstone's role in his life is never going to work.'

The cold hard certainty in his tone was enough to make Phoebe shrink lower in the sofa.

'From the moment I met you and Gladstone at the embassy I knew you were hiding something from me, Phoebe, by the way you behaved. So I had a friend of mine who heads a security agency check what you had done since you left London.'

Her mouth fell open, and she stared at him in mounting horror as he continued in a brisk tone, as though he was delivering a report.

'You returned to live with your aunt, and Ben was born seven months and one week after we parted. I had my suspicions, so I checked with Marcus earlier this week and he confirmed you had definitely had a miscarriage and lost the baby. I could not fathom how Ben could be my child until he told me he was a miracle baby. To make absolutely sure, when I left here earlier I called Marcus—who informed me it was perfectly possible, though very rare. Then I visited the cottage hospital where he was born. The receptionist there was most helpful. I asked if I could have a copy of Ben's medical notes, because you and I were taking him to Greece and needed them as a precaution in case he had an accident while there.'

Phoebe, no longer shrinking, sat up straight and placed her glass back on the table with a shaking hand, her temper rising at the thought of the arrogant swine having her checked out simply because he hadn't liked the way she behaved at a ball! Then to go to the hospital—the mind boggled! She stared at him in a bitter, hostile silence, her anger and resentment growing with every word he spoke.

'The woman was a romantic at heart, and when I told her of our tragic separation and how you and I were now reunited and intended to marry she was more than helpful. She gave me a photocopy. I know Ben was born in January, by Caesarean section and that he was two weeks overdue. I know he was one of what would have been twins—though it was clever of you to forget the name of hospital where you had the miscarriage!' He raised a mocking eyebrow. 'I also know Ben broke his arm falling out of the pear tree in your garden.'

She had not been being clever. At the time she had been afraid that if she revealed the name of the hospital that had registered her on that day somehow Jed and Dr Marcus would find out. Not surprising, given that seven weeks earlier she had lost a baby, been betrayed and dumped by the man she loved.

But she was not afraid any more, and Phoebe had heard enough. 'You had no right—the woman had no right!' she exclaimed, outraged by his revelations.

She didn't blame the receptionist. Jed was a sophisticated, strikingly handsome man who could charm the birds out of the trees if he wanted to—as she knew to her cost. She doubted there was a woman born who could resist him. That poor receptionist had never stood a chance.

'Yes, I had every right. He is *my* son and you deliberately kept him from me. If anyone had no right to do what they have done it is you. I asked you earlier why, and now I want some answers.'

The gall, the bare-faced cheek of the man—checking her out, checking the hospital out, interfering in her well-ordered life just because he could. It was all too much for Phoebe. She jumped to her feet to stare down at him, her blue eyes blazing with contempt for the heartless bastard.

'I will give you answers.' He could suck on the truth and she hoped it choked him. 'Try your own words. "A man does not expect his mistress to get pregnant." Does that ring any bells? "A child is not on my agenda,"' she quoted scathingly, before summing up for him. 'You never wanted a baby.' And she watched as a dark tide of colour swept up over his high cheekbones.

'So I panicked a little? I'm a single man, and we are programmed to believe the worst result of sex is pregnancy. I was shocked.'

'I am not an idiot—even if I did almost let you make me one. You have never panicked in your life,' Phoebe shot back. 'And nothing shocks you, Mr Bloody Invincible.' She swore—not something she often did, but she was fighting for her child. 'You were your usual super cool controlled self and you meant every word. Then, as I recall, you had the gall to tell me not to worry and that your discreet, private Dr Marcus would take care of the pregnancy and you would pay for everything. A termination was what you offered me—but lucky for you I miscarried anyway. Hardly surprising in the circumstances, and it didn't cost you a penny.'

Jed Sabbides—wealthy, powerful, confident of his place in the world, feared by some and respected by most—for once found he was speechless...

He could not believe what he was hearing. It had never entered his head when Phoebe had told him she was pregnant that she should have a termination. He had been trying to reassure her in declaring that Dr Marcus would take care of her in pregnancy. He had meant all the way through her pregnancy and beyond. But, thinking back, he realised it might not have sounded like that to Phoebe. Suddenly the comments she had made in the hospital about saving him shed-loads of money, and in the scheme of things the cost of a private doctor being nothing to him, which had puzzled him at the time made perfect sense if she believed what she did. How could they have got their wires so badly crossed? he wondered, appalled at her conclusion.

'I never suggested a termination—ever,' he murmured, but Phoebe wasn't listening.

She was looking down at him as if he was something that had crawled out from under a rock, her blue eyes blazing with passion. And that passion was pure hatred, he realised with a sense of shock. Consumed by his anger at what he saw as her betrayal, he had never considered her take on the past might differ dramatically from his—never considered the situation from her misguided view.

Phoebe was on a roll and, oblivious to Jed's stunned reaction, she felt all the fear and fury she had blanked out at the time come flooding back.

'But hey, Jed,' she quipped sarcastically, 'lucky for me you didn't turn up to take me to the clinic that next week, but instead let Christina, your PA, tell me you had discussed my miscarriage with her and inform me you weren't coming back and advise me to leave. Otherwise Ben would have been scraped out of my womb by your oh, so discreet Dr Marcus. And now you have the brass nerve to ask me why I never told you about Ben. You make me sick, turning up here and throwing your weight around, conning the hospital receptionist into giving you information with a load of lies. As for telling her we were getting married—forget it. That is *never* going to happen. Much the same way as it never happened last time when you told me you had decided we were going to be a family *after* I had lost the baby,' she added derisively. 'A simple ploy to make yourself sound good when it no longer meant anything—and you are still the same selfish, egotistical devil now, who thinks only of himself and his own wants to the exclusion of everyone else. So forgive my skepticism, but I don't believe for one minute your apparent interest in being a father, your sudden desire for a son. And I am telling you here and now. You are not getting mine...'

'Have you quite finished tearing my character to shreds?' Jed demanded, replacing the wine glass on the table and slowly rising to his feet.

He had listened with growing anger and horror as he realised he could not actually refute Phoebe's analysis of his behaviour in the past. He *had* called her a mistress and he *had* declared a child was not on his agenda—a child had not been at the time. Phoebe had dropped her pregnancy on him so casually it had been like an explosion in his head and he had been in a state of shock. But not for a second had he even thought of a termination. Later in the hospital, when he had said they would be a family, what he had meant was he would marry her—but he could see how that might have sounded hollow after the fact—and he *had* told Christina about the miscarriage.

Jed did not want to believe Phoebe's story about Christina telling her to leave the apartment, though he could not dismiss it. He had dispensed with Christina's services after she'd made it embarrassingly obvious she wanted a much more personal relationship with him. He had given Christina his cellphone that night in Greece, so it

probably was true. There were certainly enough half-truths
in everything else Phoebe had said to make him feel like
the lowest of the low—a totally alien feeling for him, a
man who prided himself on his honour and integrity.

But if the passion and the conviction in Phoebe's voice
was anything to go by she truly believed he was capable
of terminating his unborn child, and considered him the
scum of the earth. Whatever he said in his defence would
fall on deaf ears... She would never believe him now...

He pulled his mind back from the past, a grim determination tightening his jaw. The mistakes of the past could
not be changed, but that didn't deter him from wanting
his son. The only difference was he would have to change
tactics.

He let his dark eyes roam over her. She was beautiful any time, but magnificent in her passionate anger. It
reminded him of her other passion. He had lost count of
the days, the weeks, the months he had ached for her after
they parted. His gaze lingered on her heaving breasts beneath the soft cotton of her shirt and his body tightened in
arousal. Suddenly he wanted her so badly he could taste
it, and in that moment an alternative solution occurred to
him—not very ethical, but with his intimate knowledge of
Phoebe almost certainly effective...

'You have no character,' Phoebe snapped. 'And I was
finished with you years ago—or should I say you were finished with me,' she amended. 'It is too late now to change
your mind for what ever nefarious reason—and knowing
you there must be one.'

Lost in the bitter memories of the past, Phoebe had not
noticed Jed had moved to within touching distance, and
only now did she see the carefully controlled expression
on his handsome face was not reflected in the predatory
gleam in his dark eyes.

'You know me so well, Phoebe, it seems,' he drawled mockingly as his strong hands reached to curve around her shoulders.

She tensed at his touch, her heart skipping a beat and her hands curling into fists at her sides as she fought the impulse to push him away, refusing to give him the satisfaction of seeing her feminine fear at his closeness. She was immune to him and had been for years, she reminded herself.

'You are right, of course. There is a reason. I'm a very wealthy man and it has occurred to me I need a son and heir. A ready-made one seems much more preferable to a squealing baby. Thus I am confirming your low opinion of me?' Jed said, and waited…watching…testing…

Why she was disappointed Phoebe could not fathom. Jed had proved her right. She looked up at him. His dark-lashed eyes were cool on hers, and yet for a second she thought she saw a flicker of vulnerability in the inky depths and had the incredible notion he wanted her to deny his conclusion. Then she noted a nerve beating steadily beneath one sharp cheekbone in his determination to retain his formidable control, and she realised she had imagined something that was never there. Jed would be vulnerable maybe on his dying day, but not before.

Nothing had changed…Jed hadn't changed… He was an emotional bankrupt and he preferred life that way…

'Yes,' she finally responded. 'And now you understand why I didn't tell you about Ben you can leave us alone,' she told him, pleased at the cool firmness in her tone. 'Marry Sophia and make your own babies,' she tagged on for good measure.

'That might be difficult as we split up and she is not speaking to me.'

'Wise woman,' she quipped, and could not suppress a

grin. Why it pleased her to learn Jed and Sophia had parted she didn't question.

It was the grin that did it!

Jed had had enough. Talking was getting him nowhere, and Phoebe's irrepressible grin had reminded him forcibly of what he had been missing all these years. What he had thought not very ethical a minute ago no longer seemed so.

In business he had no problem playing on a rival's weakness to clinch a deal—it was accepted practice—so why not in his private life?

CHAPTER SIX

SUDDENLY Jed's strong hands tightened on her slender shoulders and Phoebe was jerked off balance. She found herself held tight against his broad chest. 'Let go of me,' she snapped, startled by his abrupt action.

'Shut up,' he growled, and before she could react he had swung her off her feet, deposited her flat on her back on the sofa and followed her down.

For a moment Phoebe was too stunned to move, and then she tried to scramble from under him. But with his great body lying half over hers, pressing her into the soft cushions, all she could do was lash out with her hands. 'Get off me!' she yelled, panicking.

He laughed—he actually laughed. And, grabbing her wrists, he pinned them above her head with one strong hand, the other cupping her chin so she could not turn her head away, and forced her to look up into his darkly handsome face.

'Are you mad? What on earth do you think you are doing?' she demanded, and tried to struggle. But with her hands captured and one long leg trapping her thighs all she could do was wriggle—and that caused her more problems, as she was suddenly vitally aware of his hard, powerful body in the most intimate way.

'Exactly what you imagine, Phoebe, because I have

nothing more to lose,' he said with a wickedly sensuous smile. 'According to you I have no character, no emotion... would you like to continue?' And he waited, his dark eyes gleaming down into hers and the hand cupping her chin stroking slowly down to her waist, edging up under her shirt.

Fury gave way to another emotion as every nerve in her body tightened and she trembled at the warmth of his hand against her bare midriff, his strong thigh pressing against her jean-clad legs. She felt his breath against her face, and then he dipped his head and brushed his lips against hers.

'Take your time in answering,' he said, and the tip of his tongue flicked out to trace the outline of her mouth. 'Though listing the negative aspects of my character may seriously damage my ego. I would much prefer to explore the positives between us,' he husked.

She shook her head in denial. She knew Jed was no longer asking her to list his character traits. If he ever had... He was asking a much more intimate question. But somehow, with the weight of him pressing against her and the familiar scent of him enfolding her, she could not find her voice—and to her shame she felt the rising heat of desire scorch though her.

'Not too much time,' he murmured against her throat, his mouth covering the suddenly heavily beating pulse there and then moving to breathe lightly against her ear. 'I don't want you to do anything you are not happy with, but this was always the best means of communication between you and I, and nothing has changed. You only have to say no and I will stop.'

Phoebe swallowed hard. The tension in the air was palpable. His dark eyes were watching her, and the hand at her midriff moved higher to cup one full firm breast, long fingers delving beneath the lacy bra to graze a taut nipple, and she could not stop the gasp of shocked pleasure escaping her lips.

She shuddered as Jed captured her mouth, his tongue slipping between her helplessly parted lips as he deepened the kiss with a skilful, gentle eroticism that was at odds with the way he had got her into this position. His long fingers caressed her breasts as he lifted his head and pressed tiny kisses over her cheeks, her brow, and then back to slip gently between her softly parted lips again.

If Jed's kisses had been like the one when he had stormed into her home she might have had the strength to fight, Phoebe realised. But they weren't. He kissed her with tenderness and gentle passion, and even as her mind told her to resist her body didn't get the message and she shuddered with an undeniable familiar need. The blood flowed thicker through her veins and she succumbed helplessly to the wonder of his kiss, to the skilful caress of his long fingers against her flesh. She was unaware he had unfastened her shirt and bra until he lowered his head to nuzzle between her breasts.

A moan rose in her throat and softly sighed between her parted lips. She knew she should stop him, and she would soon… Her body and mind were trapped between desire and despair at what was happening to her.

'You are so perfect…' Jed murmured huskily, raising his head to look into her dazed blue eyes. 'You have no idea how long I have been aching for this.' And he lowered his head to tease and lick her nipples into hard peaks of aching pleasure.

Desire won. Phoebe twisted and squirmed beneath him, consumed by a need so fierce it was almost painful a whimper of regret escaping her as he ended the torturous pleasure. He was killing her by inches and she was helpless to resist the way she felt—didn't want to…

His dark head lifted and suddenly her hands were free. She stared up into his handsome face and saw his dark eyes burn black with the effort he was making to control his passion. The same question was in their glittering depths.

'I want you, Phoebe,' he said thickly. 'I want you badly—but it is your decision,' he declared, lowering his head to press his mouth to the slender curve of her throat, mouthing dark husky words in Greek against her tender skin.

She was lost, flung back in time to when they were first lovers.

'Tell me you want me—say it, Phoebe.'

'Yes, oh, yes,' she groaned as his mouth found hers, parting her lips with a sensuality she welcomed with a need, a hunger she had no thought of denying.

Phoebe barely noticed when his fingers found the snap of her jeans. She was oblivious to everything but the musky male heat and the taste of him, and before she knew it they were naked on the huge sofa.

Her dazed gaze skimmed over the broad expanse of his tanned chest and the flood of warmth became a torrent. It had been so long since she had seen, touched his magnificent naked torso. She reached out a hand to stroke and caress his firm body, rediscovering the pleasure of tracing each muscle, the slightly abrasive feel of his soft body hair, the hard male nipples.

Jed caught her wandering hand. 'Let me look at you,' he rasped, his dark smoldering gaze raking over her face and down to the proud thrust of her breasts, the narrow waist, the flat stomach with its telltale scar, where his gaze lingered for a second, before drifting to the soft curls at the apex of her thighs.

'You are so stunningly beautiful, Phoebe,' he groaned and, lifting her hand to his lips, he pressed a kiss to the palm before letting it go.

The poignancy of the caress made Phoebe catch her breath, and she reached for him again, clasping his shoulders, digging her fingers into the firm flesh, urging him closer. But he would not be hurried.

'Exquisite,' he murmured. 'I love your hair so long.'

When she had lost her hairband Phoebe had no idea, but as his long fingers threaded through the long silken locks, erotically sweeping her hair over and around to frame her breasts, she didn't care.

Then, as Jed continued his erotic exploration, his strong hands cupping her breasts and sliding lovingly down to shape her waist, her hips, her thighs, her legs, she was swept away in a flood of sensuality so powerful she could barely breathe.

He dipped his head to lightly kiss her rigid nipples and the scar on her belly as his hands trailed back up over her inner thighs, expert fingers seeking the folds of tender flesh that guarded the centre of her femininity.

The ache, the fire deep within, burst into a flame of desire so potent she shook with the force of her need, involuntarily parting her legs as his long fingers glided between the velvet lips, teasing and tormenting the warm, wet, sensitive core until she became a slave all over again to the agonising pleasure his touch aroused, her slender body taut as a bowstring, trembling on the brink.

'So hot, so sweet and so ready,' he rasped, and withdrew the torturous caress of his fingers. His mouth trailed kisses up over her breasts, her helplessly arched throat, and finally covered her swollen lips, his tongue mimicking the act of possession before swooping lower to capture an aching nipple again to tease and suckle.

She raked her hands down his broad back in mindless need. She wanted him there between her legs, filling her... completing her...

A whimpering cry escaped as his strong hands lifted her and he eased his taut body totally over her and into the cradle of her hips. She felt the rock hard strength of him against her and squirmed as the smooth dome of his erection slid between her trembling thighs, teasing her with short, delicate strokes, rubbing against the tiny nub hidden there until she was desperate. But still he would not be hurried.

'Please,' she begged, and only then did he thrust slowly into her hot, pulsing silken centre.

She clung fervently to him, locking her long legs around his back as he lifted her higher and plunged deeper and deeper with each powerful thrust, filling her, stretching her, until the awesome power of his possession flung her into a whirlpool of spiralling passion and her whole body convulsed in a mindless paroxysmal release.

Jed's skin was drawn taut over his high cheekbones as he battled for control. He felt her lush body convulse around him, and with one last thrust his supreme effort of control was shattered as the inner muscles of her sleek, tight body drained the very essence from him in a prolonged, earth-shattering mutual climax.

Phoebe felt his full weight relax on her, his dark head buried in the curve of her neck, and with the tremors in her body finally subsiding she didn't care. Her eyes drifted closed. Languorous in the aftermath of making love, she stroked her hands lazily up his broad back, relishing the feel of his sweat-slicked skin, the heavy rasp of his breathing. It was the first time all over again—slow and tender and Jed was hers...

Her eyes flew open as the thought registered. He was not

hers—never had been. Her mind provided instant replays of their lovemaking, and she had to bite her lips to stop herself groaning. She had *begged* him to make love to her. But they had not made love—they'd had sex, nothing more. Turning her head, she settled her eyes on the fireplace and the unlit fire in the grate. She dropped her hands to her sides, suddenly chilled to the bone.

Her heart felt as dead as the unlit fire—how had it happened? She hated Jed and yet she had fallen under the spell of his sensual expertise is exactly the same way as she had years ago. She had loved him then, but now she had no excuse, and as she lay beneath him shame at her own weak-willed surrender consumed her.

The only sound in the stillness of the room was his heavy breathing.

Finally Jed eased up off her, his head propped on one elbow, a slumberous, satisfied smile gleaming his dark eyes and quirking the corners of his sensuous mouth.

'Now, *that* is what I call communicating,' he quipped, and reached a hand to flick a few tendrils of hair from her face. 'Much better than wasting time in fruitless argument that leads nowhere, don't you think, Phoebe?'

She avoided his teasing gaze. 'No, I don't think,' she murmured. That was her problem when Jed was around, she realised. He only had to look at her and she was aware of him in the most basic way. Touch her, kiss her, and she fell like a ripe plum into his lap.

Spying her jeans and shirt on the floor, she shoved at his chest, Caught off balance, he fell to the floor, but ignoring his startled yell she leapt off the sofa. Her self-respect in shreds, she gathered up her clothes and scooted across to safety behind the armchair, casting him a wary glance as she frantically pulled them on. He was naked, spread-eagled on the wood floor, and the look of astonishment on his face was priceless, but she didn't care—and she didn't care about her underwear either. She simply needed to be covered.

'Well, that is a first—being knocked to the ground.' Jed grinned. 'And not quite the response I expected,' he continued, slowly rising to his feet. 'I know you enjoyed every second of what we just shared, Phoebe—as much as I did. So surely now we can discuss the future sensibly?'

'You and I have no future. This was a mistake,' she said, and looked at him again—which was another mistake. His black hair was curling haphazardly over his brow, and the expression on his handsome face was one of amused tolerance. As for his body... Helplessly, she swept her gaze swept over him, standing tall, his great body gleaming golden in the lamplight. She had almost forgotten how good he looked stark naked—the wide shoulders and broad chest, the narrow hips, strong thighs, long legs. He took her breath away, and quickly she glanced away. 'And put some clothes on. My Aunt Jemma will be back soon,' she lied.

'You never used to be such a prude, Phoebe.' He chuckled, and strolled across to where she stood. 'Nor such a liar.'

'I do not lie,' she lied. Her head tilted back, she looked defiantly up at his darkly handsome face. She did not dare look anywhere else...

He lifted a finger and tapped her nose. 'Growing like Pinocchio's,' he pronounced. 'Because I happen to know your aunt is in Australia for two months.' He grinned again.

His good humour and confidence riled Phoebe. 'Let me guess—the hospital receptionist told you? That is the trouble with living in rural community. Everyone knows your business,' she said bitterly. 'After the story you fed her I will be fielding questions about you for months after you are gone.'

'I am not going anywhere without Ben. I have booked into the local pub for as long as it takes to persuade you. I want to take him to Greece to meet my father and the rest of the family.'

Phoebe stared up at him and saw by the expression on his handsome face that he was deadly serious, not a hint of amusement lingering in his eyes.

'That is not going to happen,' she said bravely, but inside she was quaking like a leaf with fear at the prospect of Ben going to Greece—not to mention the prospect of Jed being in her life again, especially with fresh evidence of her own demeaning response to him. Tearing her gaze away didn't help. A naked man should not be able to look so intimidating and yet so desirable. Closing her eyes for a second, she shook her head, totally humiliated by her own weakness where he was concerned. Then, opening them again, she looked straight past him.

'You have had your fun, Jed. Get dressed before you catch cold.' She spoke to him as she would to Ben, and, picking up her glass of wine from the table, she glanced at the sofa before turning to sink down into the armchair.

Phoebe felt exhausted, yet her own innate honesty forced her to admit she was more sensually alive than she had been in years. How had he got too her so quickly? she wondered. Five years of celibacy could do that to a woman, she supposed, and took a sip of wine. Especially with a super-stud like Jed Sabbides, who was fast becoming the bane of her life…

'Though on second thoughts a dose of pneumonia might get you out of my life,' she muttered.

'Not a very nice sentiment to the father of your child,

and not worthy of the Phoebe I knew, with the laughing eyes and the tender heart.'

Surprised, she glanced at him, but if he thought he could sweet-talk her simply because they'd had sex he was wasting his time. She was relieved to see he had put his jeans on, but she could not help admiring the play of muscles in his chest and abdomen as he raised his arms and pulled the black sweater over his head. As his dark head emerged he looked down at her, the knowing sensual gleam in his eyes telling her he had read her mind.

Jed was too sophisticated, too knowledgeable of the female sex. She had no doubt many more beautiful and more experienced women than her had fallen for his seductive charms. She hadn't stood a chance.

Phoebe was disgusted with herself—and him…coupling like animals on Aunt Jemma's prized sofa. Yet she could not deny the lingering warmth inside her, the musky male scent of him still in her nostrils. She shivered, suddenly afraid not just for Ben but for herself.

She had to get rid of Jed before she succumbed to his overwhelming masculine attraction all over again. She had to get rid of him once and for all—or at least limit any contact with him to the bare minimum. With that in mind, she answered him.

'You never knew me, Jed. You never wanted to—except as a willing female in your bed, eager to do anything you asked.' It took every ounce of willpower she possessed to look steadily at him. 'If you think having sex with me now changes anything, you are wrong. I am no longer the innocent girl who thought sex equated with love. You should be pleased with yourself. You taught me well. Sex is just sex—a pleasurable pastime, but never to be confused with love.'

He didn't look pleased. The dark eyes staring down at

her flared with anger and some other emotion she could not define, but she didn't care as she continued. 'I love my son. Ben is a delightful, happy and open-hearted boy, loved by those around him, and there is no way am I going to let a cold, emotionally retarded man like you come between us.'

'You seem to forget he is my son as well,' Jed prompted.

'Unfortunately I can't forget… And I concede you are right in as much as we *do* need to talk.'

'Seeing sense at last,' he stated, and moved closer.

Phoebe lifted her arm and held her hand out palm-up in rejection.

'Wait—hear me out,' she demanded, her blue eyes cold on his hard face. 'I will tell Ben you are his father when I think he is ready, and I am willing to allow you to visit him—but under my rules. The times of your visits are to be arranged sensibly between us or through a lawyer. But either way I will not allow you to take him out on his own or to Greece, simply because I don't trust you to return him.'

'You *dare* to lay down rules to me?' Jed declared, outraged. He had listened to Phoebe malign him long enough and, grasping her by the upper arms, he hauled her to her feet. 'Now it is your turn to listen to me, woman. For starters, five years ago I *never* suggested you have a termination. I was angry when you said you were pregnant because it simply wasn't something I expected and you caught me off guard. What I said later, when I had got over my initial panic, was supposed to reassure you. I told you not to worry and that Dr Marcus would look after you meaning I would provide the best medical care for your pregnancy and I would pay for everything. I meant until the child was born and ever after. So get *that* into your crazy mixed-up mind once and for all. To me, all life is sacred. I would never, ever suggest terminating a child of mine.' Jed declared adamantly.

'I know I said having a child was not on my agenda, but logically how could it be when you had only told me moments earlier you were pregnant? And if you think you can use your misguided perception of the conversation we had to prevent me claiming Ben as my son, forget it… You have had Ben to yourself for years, but not any more—of that I can assure you.' His dark eyes raked over her casually clad slender body, so feminine and yet so deceitful, Jed reminded himself.

'Now, we can do this the easy way: put the welfare of our child first by marrying and providing him with a stable home and two parents. Or we can do it the hard way and fight in every court there is for custody. That is the only choice you have, Phoebe, believe me. There is no way I am going to be a part-time father in my son's life.'

Phoebe drew in a shuddering breath. His denial of ever suggesting a termination made a kind of sense, if it was true. And trust Jed to have a logical explanation for the *not on the agenda*. Unfortunately that *did* ring true. Could she possibly have been mistaken all these years?

Either way, it did not really matter, and the *crazy mixed-up mind* comment had gone down like a lead balloon. She was slow to anger, but this arrogant man holding her had made her just that. It was Jed who drove her crazy…making her doubt herself. But there was absolutely no doubt in her mind that he had deserted her in the end. Whatever excuse he came up with could not change that fact.

Now he had walked back into her life, into her house, and in no time at all had seduced her into having sex. And she had let him, almost begged him. Worst of all, he had made her afraid.

She had fought hard to build her self-esteem after Jed's betrayal, to build a life and a career to support her son, and she was proud of what she had achieved. No way would she allow his incredibly powerful personality to overcome her own. She had once before and it had almost destroyed her.

Phoebe stared defiantly up at him and, avoiding the termination issue, latched on to his last comment. 'You won't be able to help it,' she derided. 'I seem to remember you were always a workaholic, flying between continents on business every few days. I once worked out that in our twelve-month affair we actually spent less than six months together. Unless you have had a massive lifestyle change you would always be a part-time father, married or not, and as I have told you I prefer *not*.'

Jed stiffened, dropping his hands to curl them into fists at his sides as he looked at her long and hard. Then his heavy lidded eyes lowered, masking his expression.

'No, I have not changed, Phoebe,' he finally responded. 'But you certainly have. You rarely argued with me before. I remember a beautiful, bright and sensual girl, eager to explore all life had to offer. Not a sharp-tongued—'

'You mean a besotted fool,' she cut in swiftly. 'Willing to do your bidding at the drop of a hat. Well, those days are well and truly over. I am a mother—I have a son I love and a life that I love, and we don't need you. I want you to leave now.' Suddenly she was tired, confused, and just wanted him gone.

'Don't worry, I will. But before I leave you need to hear a few home truths—something to think about before I return tomorrow,' he told her curtly. 'Whatever you may think, Ben does need me. However much you try to deny it, the boy is part Greek. He is going to inherit a major Greek company one day, and a lot more. He needs to know the language and how to handle the responsibility—not something he is likely to learn stuck in a quiet backwater of the English countryside with a mother and great-aunt his only family.'

Phoebe listened in growing alarm as a stony-faced Jed continued in a cold, hard tone. 'I remember you told me your parents died in a car accident when you were seventeen. But Ben has a grandfather, an aunt and uncle, cousins, and a dozen other relatives in Greece—not to mention a father,' he declared with an arrogant arch of one ebony brow. 'Do you really think he will thank you later for depriving him of the largest part of his family?' he queried. 'Or is it more likely he will grow to resent you for depriving him of what is his by right?'

With a sinking heart Phoebe realised what Jed said could very well be true. *Did* she have the right to deprive Ben of the Greek side of his family? In her heart she knew the answer was no, and the realisation sapped what little energy she had left. All she wanted to do was go to bed and bury her head under the pillow, pretend today had never happened, but she knew that was not an option.

'You may be right,' she sighed, too exhausted to argue further.

'You know I am, Phoebe,' he drawled, his eyes no longer cold as they met hers. Something in the gleaming depths made her heart miss a beat. 'You may think you have the ideal life with Ben, but there is nothing ideal about bringing up a child without a father. Even a part-time one, as you think I would be.' He lifted his hand and drew a gentle finger down her cheek. 'But given a chance I could surprise you.'

Jed did… His hand slipped lower down to curve round her waist, and with his eyes still locked with hers, the warmth in them unmistakable, he bent his head and brushed her lips with his. He kissed her softly, gently, before raising his head, a wry smile on his handsome face.

'What was that for?' Phoebe asked, stirred by his tenderness when she did not want to be.

'For Ben, and for what we shared in the past—and for what we just shared now on your very accommodating sofa. I could not leave you in anger. Sit and finish your drink. I'll see myself out.'

Phoebe was left staring at his broad back as he walked out of the room. She was still standing when she heard the front door softly close. Only then did she sink back down into the armchair. Picking up her glass of wine, she drained it.

Damn! She was mindlessly obeying Jed again…and swearing was in danger of becoming a habit with her all because of him.

She glanced wearily around, her gaze alighting on the sofa. It was impossible to miss it, dominating the room, but she would never be able to sit on it again without remembering her downfall—and Jed.

Amazingly, with all the anger, fear and humiliation she felt at her own weakness where he was concerned, a smile curled her kiss-swollen lips as she saw again in her mind Jed's big body sprawled on the floor, and the look of total confusion on his face as to how he had got there—identical to Ben's when he had a fall. Jed had looked funny, and he had surprised her because instead of being angry, as she had expected, he'd been amused…

He had surprised her also with his adamant denial that he had suggested a termination. For years she'd believed that he had, and had used it to cling to her hatred of him, but now she was forced to face the fact she was probably wrong. He had never actually said the word. All she had heard was that Dr Marcus would 'take care' of her pregnancy and that Jed would pay for everything, and in her emotional state, with her innocent fantasy of a ring and marriage so brutally squashed, maybe she had been thinking a bit wildly and put the worst connotation on his statement…

Not that what she had thought made any difference now.

Jed was here and he wanted his son, and she had to deal with him.

CHAPTER SEVEN

PHOEBE barely slept, and when she did a tall dark man haunted her dreams. She awoke with a start to find Ben standing by the bed. She glanced at the clock—six-thirty in the morning. Watching Ben scramble up on to the bed, demanding she get up, she laughed and gave him a cuddle—but inside she was worried sick at the thought of how his young life might change with the arrival of Jed Sabbides.

As for her life—the very idea of Jed sweeping in and out of it for heaven knew how long didn't bear thinking about. Having to see him on a regular basis visiting Ben was not something she looked forward too, but after a long, restless night she realised she would eventually have to give Jed more than supervised visiting rights to his son. Subjecting Ben to a custody battle was a pointless exercise. As his mother, she had no doubt she would win full custody, but the courts would certainly give Jed partial rights anyway. The only alternative offered—to marry the man—was completely out of the question. She had trusted Jed once with her heart and soul, and he had destroyed her trust. A marriage might work without love if there was respect and friendship between the couple, but without trust there was no hope.

Phoebe would never trust Jed again, and she could think of no hell on earth worse than being married to a man her own innate honesty forced her to admit she had little to no power to resist on a sexual level. That was something else she had learned last night as she awoke from a dream, her body hot and throbbing with frustration.

For years, sex or the lack of it had not bothered her—yet Jed in no time at all had reduced her to a sensually needy female with an ease that scared her. No way was she putting her head in *that* noose again.

In that moment Phoebe made her decision. She would tell Jed she was willing to amend the conditions on his visiting rights and allowing him to see Ben. At first it would be in her presence, but later, once Ben was comfortable with him, on his own. It was a big concession on her part, which meant eventually gifting Jed a modicum of trust, but not yet—and she wasn't going to tell him today...

Today she was going to take Ben to the caravan they owned at a holiday park on the edge of Weymouth Bay. They spent all their holidays there and Ben loved the place. They could pick up the wallpaper for his bedroom in the home decor shop in Weymouth, and over the weekend go searching for fossils at Lyme Regis before closing the caravan up for the winter. The autumn half term holiday was usually the last time they used the caravan until the next year. She wasn't really running away...

Maybe it was cowardly, Phoebe admitted, but she did not feel like facing Jed again quite so soon—not after so helplessly falling apart in his arms last night. She needed time to regain her emotional balance, and this was the perfect solution. At least she could avoid him for a couple of days.

Her car was parked at the end of the drive, the case with their clothes was in the boot, and they were almost ready to leave.

Phoebe glanced around. It was beautiful crisp autumn morning, the sun was shining, and she took a deep breath, her spirits rising. She was warmly dressed in a blue ribbed wool sweater and grey trousers, her cashmere jacket was already in the car, and she glanced at her son.

'Right, Ben, have you got everything? Rucksack and wellies for the beach?' she prompted, and she smiled as he held up his bright red wellington boots and bag. 'Good—put them in the car, and then we can go.' Holding open the rear passenger door, she watched as he tightened his grip on the boots in one hand and the small rucksack containing tools and toys in the other.

Suddenly the roar of a car engine shattered the silence and she froze, but with a glance up the road she recognised Julian's red Ferrari and heaved a sigh of relief. The car drew to a growling halt and Julian leapt out and strolled towards her, a broad grin on his attractive face.

'Hi, Phoebe—Ben my favourite godson.' He gave Ben a high five. 'Going fossil-hunting I see.' It was Julian who had introduced Ben to the hobby, and given him the small rucksack with the child-sized tools.

'Yes.' Ben grinned happily up at Julian, and then moved to place his things on the floor of the car.

'How are you, Phoebe?' Julian asked, his silver gaze resting on her.

'Fine.' She smiled as he looped an arm around her shoulders.

'You don't look it. Dark circles under the eyes…what have you been up to?' he joked.

'Nothing m—' But the roar of another car engine drowned out her response.

Unbelievable. She groaned as the black Bentley coming from the opposite direction swerved across the road to pull up a foot in front of the Ferrari, effectively blocking her drive.

Jed Sabbides was not in the best of moods. The first call he had made after discovering Ben was definitely his son yesterday had been to Leo, the head of the security firm that guarded the Sabbides family, to arrange for his operative Sid in England to watch over Phoebe and Ben—with a few added precautions. One of which had been to inform him if they left their home. He had no intention of letting Phoebe run out on him again. Which was why, when he'd received the call this morning in the middle of breakfast, he had left immediately. And had arrived, from what he could see, just in time.

Phoebe, with her long hair swept back in a ponytail and wearing a figure hugging blue jumper and grey pants, looked stunning, and his body reacted with instant enthusiasm even as he frowned at the sight of her companion.

What the hell was Julian Gladstone doing here so early? And with his arm around Phoebe... Whatever they'd had going before, Jed did not want to know. But as of last night Phoebe was his again, and the sooner the man understood that the better.

He let none of his anger show as he stopped his car and got out.

Phoebe tensed, her blue eyes widening as Jed exited the car. Cleanshaven, he was wearing the same black leather jacket as yesterday, and underneath a white rollneck sweater. His long legs were encased in blue denim jeans, and if anything he looked more wickedly attractive than he ever had before. Maybe because a vivid image of him standing in the middle of her living room, his great body stark naked, his bronzed skin gleaming moist in the aftermath of sex, flashed inconveniently into her mind...

Julian bent his blond head to murmur in her ear. 'Ah,

now I understand the dark circles.' Straightening, he called
out in his cut-glass English accent as Jed walked towards
them. 'Good morning. Jed Sabbides, I believe. You are a
long way from home, old man.'

Phoebe was expecting fireworks as Jed approached, but
she could not have been more wrong. He stopped a foot in
front of them.

'Hi, Phoebe.' He gave her a brief frowning glance before
dropping gracefully to his haunches and adding, 'Hello,
Ben,' his frown vanishing as he grinned at the boy.

Phoebe glanced down at the two heads almost on a level
and heard her son's joyful response. Her gaze wandered
to where the faded denim of Jed's jeans was pulled taught
across muscular thighs, outlining his sex in stark detail.
Hastily she looked away, appalled at where her thoughts
were taking her, and was relieved when Jed stood up and
turned his attention to Julian.

'Good morning, Julian Gladstone, isn't it?' He returned
Julian's greeting.

For a long moment Phoebe simply stared at the scene
before her. They were like two stags at bay—both big,
powerful males, leaders of the pack. She recognised the
macho confrontation. But then to her amazement Jed held
out his hand to Julian, who automatically slipped his arm
from her shoulders and took the offered hand.

Jed nodded his head in the direction of the road.

'Nice car you have there, Gladstone—the latest model
Ferrari.'

To Phoebe's astonishment, both men turned to admire
the red car.

'I took delivery of the same model two weeks ago, but I
have not had a chance to drive it yet. How does it handle?'
Jed asked.

For the next five minutes Phoebe might as well have

been invisible, and in one way she was grateful. Jed's brief hello had told her clearer than more words that making love—no, not love, having sex—last night meant nothing to him, whereas she, for some inexplicable reason, after years of celibacy never bothering her, had only to look at the man to start thinking about sex...

The tableau was surreal, and she shook her head to dispel her wayward thoughts and simply watched, speechless, as Julian and Jed, with her beloved Ben in tow, strolled to the side of the road. Ben was allowed to sit in the passenger seat of the Ferrari while the men entered into a serious discussion—she presumed on the relative merits of the cars.

By the time they returned to her Jed and Julian appeared to be friends, and Ben had a serious case of dual hero-worship...

'Mum, Jed has a new Ferrari the same as Uncle Julian's at his home in Greece. Do you think we can have a new car soon?' her son asked, casting a disdainful look which reminded Phoebe startlingly of his father at her old Mini Cooper and then a hopeful look up at her.

'Yes, of course you can. I'll buy a new one,' Jed answered before Phoebe could open her mouth. 'I gave that car to your mum for Christmas long before you were born. I'm amazed she still has it.' He gave Phoebe a mocking smile that was enough to make her blood pressure rise along with her anger.

'Did you really?' Julian inserted. 'You never told me that, Phoebe.' And after a shrewd glance at the two adults he finally grinned. 'Obviously I had it wrong about you two.' Patting Ben on the head, he said, 'Have a good time, sport, I'll see you later. And good luck Jed.' Then his blue eyes held Phoebe's for a moment. 'Have a good day, Phoebe. I'll be in touch.' And he left.

Reeling in shock that first Ben and now Julian had fallen for Jed's easy charm, Phoebe bitterly resented the fact—never mind his revelation about her car and his audacity in saying he would provide a new one.

'What did you say to Julian?' she demanded of the tall dark figure beside her.

'I told him the truth—I spent an informative and intimate evening with you last night—and thanked him for being a good godfather to Ben.' Jed shrugged his broad shoulders.

He didn't see the need to inform Phoebe of everything they had discussed. Julian had been hostile at first, and had brought up his wanting Phoebe to terminate her pregnancy. Jed had told him bluntly exactly what he had actually said to Phoebe at the time. He had then suggested man to man that the mind of a woman was a mystery to most logically minded males, and the interpretation they could put on a few words might be totally illogical and contrary to what a guy actually meant. Julian had agreed with him, but somehow Jed knew repeating the conversation to Phoebe would almost certainly end with her calling him a male chauvinist pig again, and he didn't need the hassle.

He had enough of a problem trying to persuade her to his way of thinking as it was. He had thought last night their sexual compatibility would do the trick, but no such luck. He realised she did not trust him an inch, and until she did he was never going to get Ben.

Last night he had called his British lawyer and told him the whole story, and Phoebe's take on it. In his opinion Jed had little chance of winning custody of his son in an English court unless he could prove she was a totally incompetent mother—which from what Jed had told him she was not. She was a respected schoolteacher, financially viable, who owned her own home and had an aunt as a built-in babysitter. Jed didn't have a leg to stand on. The lawyer's advice was to reach an amicable arrangement with Phoebe if possible, and if not then to get the pair of them to Greece. He stood a much better chance in a Greek court.

With the lawyer's advice in mind, Jed had formed a plan to spend as long as it took with Phoebe and behave like an old friend rather than a lover while getting to know his son. Provided he could keep his hands off Phoebe, his no-sex, friendly but firm ploy would work. He knew she wanted him, and once he got her to trust him a little it should be no problem getting her to visit Greece and agree to marry him. If not, he'd go to court...

With that in mind, he wasn't going to give her the chance to argue. 'Phoebe, you go and get the things you need out of your car and put them in mine, while I put Ben in his seat. He's told me we are going out for the day, and my car will be much more comfortable for all of us.' Jed gave her a brief smile and saw the fury in her eyes. Looking down at Ben, he added, 'Isn't that right, Ben?' He wasn't above using his son to back him up, and, taking the boy's hand, he headed for the car.

Phoebe, her face scarlet with embarrassment and anger, simply stood open-mouthed at the turn of events. She was mortified at the thought of Jed implying to Julian they'd had sex, and furious at his arrogant assumption he could take over her plans for the day. At least he obviously assumed it was just for the day, which was lucky for her—because with Ben skipping along at Jed's side towards the car, his hand trustingly in the man's, she knew she could not argue with him.

Fighting with Jed in front of her son would only result in Ben resenting her interference. Maybe that was what Jed was hoping for? Biting her lip, she retrieved her jacket, the rucksack and wellington boots from her car, and, thankful for small mercies, ignored the suitcase in the boot and locked the car. She closed the gates behind her and slid into the back seat of the convertible without saying a word. Then to her horror Ben piped up…

'Mum, you've forgotten the case with all our stuff for the weekend.'

Jed glanced over his shoulder, his dark gaze narrowed. 'I thought you had planned just a day out? Ben said we are going hunting for dinosaurs—not something I have done before. But the whole weekend sounds much better. Where exactly were you planning on staying?' he demanded silkily.

'In our caravan by the sea. You can stay with us if you like. Can't he, Mum?' Ben spoke up yet again, and for the first time in her life Phoebe felt like strangling her own son.

'No, Ben we are only going for the day now,' she said through gritted teeth. 'Jed is a very important man, and we could not possibly impose on his valuable time for more than a few hours,' she said, sarcasm lacing her tone as she shot her nemesis a filthy look. 'We are wasting time. Drive on.' But he didn't

'No, Phoebe. I could not possibly deprive you of a weekend away. I have time to spare and would love to spend it with you both.'

'Isn't that great, Mum?' Ben asked, and after her brilliant son had informed Jed the caravan was huge, with two bedrooms and a sofa that made a bed, she did not even have the excuse that there was no room for the manipulative devil. Mentioning that Jed had not packed was a waste of time, as the damn man said he could buy anything he needed…

Then with a cynical smile he insisted on taking her car keys and retrieving the suitcase from her car. Phoebe, running out of excuses to refuse, was stunned into horrified silence.

Short of dragging her son out of the car and telling the hateful man to get lost she had no choice but to go along with the pair of them.

How in heaven's name, she asked herself, had her planned escape from Jed ended up with him spending the whole weekend with them—in the caravan of all places?

It would be one hell of a culture shock for the stinking rich Greek, that was for sure. She doubted he even knew what a caravan was…

He looked at her in the rearview mirror, his dark eyes gleaming with laughter. 'Right, Phoebe, where are we going and which way?' he demanded with a broad smile.

For an instant she was reminded of the first time they'd met, and the brilliance of his smile that had so captivated her. Her lips quirked at the corners in the beginnings of a smile, but she clenched her teeth instead as she realised he had good reason to smile, but she did not. Jed had got his own way yet again…

'Weymouth,' she said abruptly. 'Your sat-nav will guide you.' And, turning her head, she looked out of the window and tried to ignore him.

A while later the big car finally stopped in front of the barrier at the entrance to the caravan park.

'Wait here while I check in at Reception and get the pass.'

Phoebe had endured an hour of near silence, which unfortunately had given her a lot of time for her gaze to stray to the back of Jed's head and remember running her fingers through his thick black hair and a lot more last night. Consequently she was hot and bothered, and could not get out of the car fast enough.

Five minutes later Phoebe returned and handed the pass to Jed through the open window of the car.

'What took you so long?' he asked.

'It is Saturday morning and next week is the half term holiday—the last school break before Christmas. That is why it is busy,' she snapped.

'Ah, I understand. Jump in and tell me which way to go—I want to see where we are sleeping tonight.'

His comment, and the sensual curl of his lips as he smiled, made Phoebe's temperature almost reach boiling point, and she slid in to the back seat silently fuming.

Her temper did not improve when they reached the caravan and Jed deftly parked the car alongside. Within seconds he had lifted Ben out and ascended the steps to the balcony, waiting impatiently for her to open the door.

Instructing Ben to unpack his bag in his usual bedroom, she tried to persuade Jed to leave—telling him straight that she did not want him there, and that a man like him, accustomed to luxury, would hate the place. But all to no avail. He astounded her by saying he had driven across America in a Winnebago in his youth, and this was bigger.

With Ben running in on the argument, grabbing Jed's hand and insisting on showing him around, she had to give up...

Contrary to Phoebe's expectations, the day was not a complete disaster. After lunch in a fish restaurant on the harbour, the afternoon had been good. They had driven out to Portland Bill to see the lighthouse and take the tour of Portland Castle, and Jed had taken countless photos with his cellphone—one great one of Ben sitting astride a cannon.

But that had been after she had got over a nasty shock when they went shopping in the morning—and if she was honest one hell of a wake-up call...

Ben hadn't been able to decide which wallpaper he liked best, and had demanded both cars and dinosaurs. She had agreed, though she knew to adult eyes two walls decorated in one print and two in another was not ideal.

Jed had asked the shop-owner when they would do the work, suggesting that afternoon and evening would be good. What had happened next opened her eyes once and for all to the wealth and power of the man.

Phoebe had given Jed a condescending smile and told him the *shop* did not do the decorating—she was going to do it herself next week. But he had simply looked at her and said, 'Don't be ridiculous.' A few telephone calls later he was demanding her house keys and handing them over to a burly-looking man called Sid, along with the bags...

Apparently Sid was her son's bodyguard, as of yesterday, and he was going to stay at her home to take care of things while the decorators did their work over the weekend. The timing was ideal.

Now, showered and changed into a blue velour V-necked jumpsuit, Phoebe sat on the bed watching her sleeping son and was forced to face that, no matter how much she protested over the idea of a bodyguard, Ben's life was changed for ever. Jed had simply pointed out that Ben was his son and the fear of kidnap was an ever-present threat. That had shut her up...

Leaning forward, she brushed a few curls from his brow and dropped a soft kiss on his cheek. Standing up, she squared her shoulders and quietly left the bedroom.

CHAPTER EIGHT

Phoebe looked along the small corridor that opened out into the kitchen-dining area and the living area and, taking a deep breath, walked forward.

A large soft-cushioned seating arrangement in cream and brown was fitted the whole length of one wall, and curved a few feet each side. The middle portion folded down into a double bed if needed. A glass-topped coffee table was in the centre, and on the other wall was a neat stone-effect electric fire. Comfortable and practical—but nothing like the sort of surroundings Jed was accustomed to, she thought dryly.

But, seeing Jed sprawled along one end of the sofa, minus his shoes and with his mobile phone to his ear, talking in rapid if muted Greek, the expression on his face one of intense concentration, she saw he looked surprisingly at home.

Jed, as if sensing her approach, finished his call and lifted his head, his dark eyes resting on her. 'Ben asleep?' he asked.

'Yes. Please don't interrupt your phone calls on my account. I'm going to make a cup of tea and go to bed.'

'It is only eight, Phoebe, and avoiding the issue of Ben will not make it go away. Come and join me in a glass of

champagne and try behaving like the intelligent woman
you are instead of running scared all the time.'

It was only then that she noticed a bottle of champagne
and two glasses standing on the unit that ran under the
front window. 'Where did you get that from?'

'From the fridge in the car. We have more important
things to talk about. Ben is our son and you have done a
great job raising him. He is a bright, intelligent and loving
boy all because of you, but he does need his father—more
and more the older he gets. There will never be a better
time than now to discuss his future.'

Rising to his feet, he opened the bottle of champagne
with a quick twist, avoiding any explosive bang, and filled
the two glasses. 'You know I am right.'

He handed a glass to her and fatalistically she took it,
carefully avoiding touching his fingers with hers.

'I have no intention of pouncing on you, Phoebe,' he
drawled sardonically. 'Well, not unless I am asked.' His lips
twisted in the briefest of smiles. 'Come and sit down and
relax,' he ordered, and lounged back down on the sofa.

He was right…as usual…and there was no point in
avoiding the inevitable conversation any longer. She accepted that. As for relaxing—much to her chagrin she knew
that was beyond her. She was too intensely aware of Jed.
The close confines of the caravan did not help, but short
of perching on one of the dining chairs Phoebe had no
choice but to sit beside him—leaving a good two feet of
space between them.

'Cheers,' he said, raising his glass to hers.

Reluctantly she touched it with hers. 'Cheers,' she murmured and took a sip.

'Now, isn't that better? A toast to old times between two
friends.'

'I suppose so.' Except Jed had never truly seen her as

a friend, only as a mistress... A willing woman to share his bed and a convenient sex partner, but not good enough share his real life. He had taken great care to make sure she never met his family or mixed with any of his high-echelon friends like the ambassador and Sophia—the sophisticated elite of Greek society—and she never would be. She had to remember that he was here for her son, nothing more.

Jed noted Phoebe's hesitation and the shadow that clouded her brilliant eyes. He could tell something in what he had said had evoked a bitter memory of the past, though for the life of him he did not know why. But he wasn't taking any chances.

'This is an okay caravan—how long have you owned it?' he asked, deciding to get her into a mellow mood before laying down the law.

'Hardly up to your luxury standard!' Phoebe quipped, arching a delicate eyebrow in his direction, not fooled for a moment by his change of subject. 'But it is perfect for us,' she stated, deciding to go along with him—anything to delay the inevitable argument over Ben. 'We actually rented a caravan here for eight weeks the summer we had the two cottages converted into one. Ben was eighteen months old and he loved it by the sea so much Aunt Jemma and I decided to buy a caravan for our own use. We spend all our holidays here, and quite a few weekends,' she said, taking another sip of champagne.

'I can see Ben loves it by the sea.' Jed glanced at her, his deep brown eyes smiling into hers. 'I had a great time today with you both. I am not sure fish and chips for lunch is a healthy diet, but I enjoyed them.'

'Yes, I noticed,' Phoebe murmured, warmed by his smile in more ways than one. Hastily she took another swallow of champagne. 'Ben loves going to the fish restaurant on the harbour, and the pizzeria here on site as well—though there is also a restaurant we could have gone to.' She was beginning to ramble, and took another gulp of champagne and then drained the glass.

Jed refilled Phoebe's glass, knowing from past experience she had no head for alcohol. After a couple of glasses of champagne she would relax and be much more amiable to his plan for Ben's future. Underhand, maybe, but nowhere near as underhand as she had been in her efforts to deprive him of his son.

'You wore him out, which is some accomplishment.' Phoebe sank further back in the seat and, taking another sip of champagne, glanced sidelong at Jed. 'Actually, you surprised me. You were very good with him, and he seems to like you.'

Jed regarded her silently for a long moment. She had no idea how condescending she sounded. Contrary to popular belief that men did not bond as quickly with their child as women, from the moment he had met Ben he had immediately felt a connection so intense it had surprised him. To have Phoebe say Ben *seemed* to like him actually stung—though he supposed he should be grateful she was prepared to concede that much after trying to deny he was his father altogether.

'Thank you for that, Phoebe.' If she recognised the sarcasm in his tone it did not show, and he continued in a softer vein. 'But I have had plenty of practice with my sister's children. She has four now—two girls and two boys. When Ben comes to Greece I know his cousins will be thrilled, and his Aunt Cora and Uncle Theo will adore him. As for my father—who recently divorced his fourth wife and hopefully his last—' he grimaced '—seeing Ben will make his life complete.'

Jed saw the flicker of doubt, confusion in her eyes before she quickly lowered her gaze and took another sip of champagne. She glanced back up at him through the thick curl of her lashes and he saw something else. She was as intensely aware of him as he was of her, however much she tried to pretend otherwise. For a moment he wanted to just cut the talk and kiss her senseless. But sex was one thing he could take or leave if he had to. His son was something else entirely. Now he had found Ben he was determined to keep him—preferably with Phoebe, but if not he was going to have Ben anyway...

'Yes, well...' Phoebe murmured.

Jed talking about his family was bittersweet. When they'd been together before he had mentioned his sister and her two girls once, and told her his mother had died when he was a teenager, but she had no idea his father had been married four times. In fact she knew very little about him really, other than that he was great in bed, she thought, her blue eyes roaming over his attractive face, lingering on his mobile mouth. Involuntarily she licked her lips, remembering the heady pleasure of his kisses. She felt the increased throb of her pulse through her whole body and swiftly lowered her gaze to the half-empty glass in her hand, shamed by her helpless lust for Jed.

'Maybe some day,' she muttered, afraid to look at him. Afraid he would recognise how she was feeling. She watched as he topped up her glass and put his own down on the table.

'*Maybe* is not good enough, Phoebe,' Jed declared, and she took a long drink of champagne to steady her racing pulse. 'I want him to know his Greek family. It is unfair to Ben and unfair to me. He needs to know I am his father, and tomorrow I am going to tell him—whether you like it or not. It would be much better to agree on the moment between us, here and now.'

Obviously she was wrong. Jed had no idea her thoughts

had wandered into the erotic. He wasn't interested in her half as much as in her son, as his last statement proved. She stared up into his glittering eyes and saw the determination in the dark depths. A shiver of fear slithered down her spine. She took another great gulp of champagne and it gave her the confidence to deny him.

'No, I think you are being a bit premature. Ben needs time to get to know you—to adjust.'

Jed had had enough of playing it cool. It wasn't getting him anywhere. 'Premature… That is rich, coming from you.' His tone dripped sarcasm. 'A woman who was apparently quite happy to let Ben grow up believing his father was unknown. How do you think that makes me feel?' he demanded. 'It was sheer coincidence we met again, and it was only your inability to keep the panic out of your eyes that made me suspect something. But not for a second did I think it was my child you were hiding. I can see he is well taken care of, but instead of two women working to support him *I* should have been supporting him. I believe in taking care of my own.'

Phoebe's lips twitched. 'Don't beat yourself up over it. You have been in a way.' She giggled.

'You think this is a laughing matter—and what do you mean, in a way? he demanded starkly.

'Simple. The jewellery you gave me funded my teacher training, and that ostentatious diamond necklace alone allowed me to buy the cottage next to my aunt's. The rest bought this caravan. So you see you have nothing to feel guilty about on the monetary front.' Promptly she hiccupped, then added, 'Though on the moral front paying for sex with jewels is definitely sleazy. But, hey—according to you I had earned them, so I kept them and spent them.'

Ignoring her last comment—he had never really thought

of Phoebe that way, but he wasn't going to argue—Jed glanced around the caravan.

'You actually sold the presents I gave you?'

He pictured the converted cottage and was stunned to think the things he had given her, the cost of which had been a mere drop in the ocean to him, had helped support Phoebe in her career and everything else for five years. He spent more in a month.

'Yes. Well, most of them.'

Unable to help himself, Jed looped an arm around her waist and, catching her chin between his thumb and fingers, tilted her face to his. Her blue eyes sparkled as she gave him a brilliant smile.

'I kept the hairclip for a rainy day.'

The champagne had certainly loosened her tongue, Jed realized. She would probably never have told him the truth stone-cold sober. It made him feel a lot better, knowing he had provided something for Ben—although unwittingly.

'You didn't have to tell me that, but I'm glad that you did.' Unable to resist the temptation, he brushed his lips gently against hers.

'My pleasure,' she murmured as long lashes fluttered down over her blue eyes.

Her head fell back against the curve of his shoulder, exposing her slender throat, and her hand dropped on to his thigh. He tensed, raising his head to let his dark gaze roam over her delicate features and lower, to where her breasts were outlined by the blue velvet V-neck top she wore. The ache in his groin he had been fighting all day intensified.

Phoebe looked up at him, all soft and willing, her lips slightly parted, and he could not resist lowering his head again and licking the lush outline of her mouth, before allowing his tongue to dip inside and lightly stroke hers.

Then he withdrew to trail kisses down the elegant length of her throat.

'I swore I would not do this again.'

Phoebe was beguiled by the lazy gentle kiss and the caress, but Jed's huskily drawled comment penetrated the champagne-induced fog in her brain. Suddenly she realised his arm was around her shoulders and she was curled up against him, her hand on his leg, her slender fingers massaging a muscular thigh.

For the life of her she could not understand how she had got herself in this position yet again with a man she had despised and feared for the past five years. Too much champagne, that was how…

'You are not doing anything,' she said, struggling to sit up and swiftly removing her hand from his thigh. 'In fact you can take yourself off to a hotel. I don't trust you here.' She moved along the seat, out of his reach. She didn't dare stand up as she felt a little dizzy. She hoped from the champagne rather than from his kiss.

'You don't trust yourself, Phoebe, and I am going nowhere. But don't worry—I will be strong for both of us.'

Jed's amused drawl infuriated her, and getting to her feet she stared at him. 'The middle of the sofa folds down. There's linen on the table to make up the bed. I am going to mine, and I don't want to see or hear you until tomorrow morning, you conceited, arrogant pig.'

Jed let her go…

Picking up his mobile phone, he flicked through the photos he had taken during the day and smiled. His son… Benjamin… The knowledge was still new, but the steely glint in his eyes as he came to the end of the pictures was not. Irrespective of Phoebe, whatever it took Ben was family and he was going to live with *him*…

He glanced at the time before switching to his messages.

Ten in the evening—when had he ever gone to bed so early? he mused. The last time he'd actually spent the whole night with Phoebe. Not a good night to remember. The sex had been incredible, but the morning after had been a disaster.

He caught up with his calls, and then, connecting his laptop to a secure wireless network, worked solidly for the next three hours. A few problems had arisen that he was going to have to attend to in person in London, he realised as he finally signed off. He had not been out of the office for so long in years, and before that he had not been concentrating but wondering about Phoebe. Now he knew the incredible truth he was energised and itching to get back to work—and with a son and heir he had an added incentive.

He wasn't wasting any more time trying to talk sensibly to Phoebe. Tomorrow he was going to tell Ben he was his father and take it from there. The sexy, malleable girl of twenty-one had morphed into an even sexier, sophisticated but stubborn woman. He could wait. She would come round to his way of thinking in the end—in his experience women always did.

He was not a conceited man, but endowed with looks, brains and wealth—especially wealth—he had never met a woman yet who would not jump to marry him given half a chance. Phoebe was no different. The lure of a life of luxury would eventually overcome any scruples she might have. But he was not waiting for his son.

Phoebe woke up and groaned for a moment, not sure where she was. She forced open her eyes and realised she was at the caravan, and as the memory of yesterday surfaced she groaned again.

Another day with Jed was not something she wanted to

contemplate. She'd had as much as she could stand from the man, even though her wayward body seemed to delight in making a liar out of her.

She sat up in bed and glanced at her wristwatch. Nine in the morning. It couldn't be... Ben was always awake at the crack of dawn. Her first thought was that he must be ill. Swinging her legs over the side of the bed, she was about to stand up when Ben burst in.

'Great—you're up, Mum. Jed said I had to let you sleep, but you have been asleep for *ages*. We have been down to the café on the seafront and had breakfast and everything.'

'You should have called me. You know you must not go anywhere without telling me.' She was terrified at the thought Jed had taken Ben. He could have driven Ben off to heaven knew where—her worst nightmare...

'Jed said it was fine, because you were tired and needed a rest.'

Phoebe looked down at her son and saw the worried look in his eyes. She forced a smile 'Yes, it was okay—but don't do it again without telling me, hmm?' Planting a kiss on his brow, she straightened her shoulders, silently cursing the damn man.

Only to find Jed was now standing at the foot of her bed.

'Good morning, Phoebe. I hope you slept well?' he drawled in a deep husky tone, his dark eyes roaming over her with blatant masculine appreciation.

She swallowed hard and felt her breasts tighten beneath her top. He looked so gorgeously male, wearing jeans and a blue sweater, and suddenly she was terribly conscious of the short pyjamas she wore.

'Yes,' she muttered, pink-cheeked with embarrassment and unable to look him in the eye. She tried to straighten the clinging cotton top, but only succeeded in revealing her burgeoning nipples.

'Mum, Mum—you will never guess!'

She was glad to turn her attention to Ben. 'Guess what?' she asked.

'Jed told me at breakfast I have a daddy, and he knows where he is.'

Her clothing or lack of it faded into insignificance at his statement.

For a second Phoebe closed her eyes, her pink cheeks draining to a deathly shade of pale, and she wished the ground would open and swallow her up—or preferably Jed Sabbides. She had known some day she would have to explain to Ben more fully about his father—her aunt had warned her often enough—but not like this, being forced into it. She opened her eyes to find Ben staring at her, positively buzzing with excitement. Slowly tilting back her head, she stared up at Jed.

'It came up in conversation, Phoebe, and I would not lie to the boy. But I did say we had to ask your permission first.'

She met his not so innocent gaze, her blue eyes sparking with anger. 'Big of you. Now, would you mind leaving while I dress?'

'But I want to know where my dad is *now*.'

Ben was adamant, and though it wasn't the way she would have chosen to tell him there was no way was she letting Jed do it for her.

Pride and anger stiffened her spine, and, lifting Ben onto her lap, she stroked a few wayward curls from his brow.

'You know I said you didn't have a father because we had parted long before you were born? Well, Jed knows where your father is because *he* is your father, Ben, and he found us.'

Ben looked solemnly up at Jed. 'Are you really my daddy?'

'Yes, Ben. Your mum and I lost touch, and I had no idea you existed until Friday, when we met again and to my joy I discovered you were my son. I promise we will never lose each other again.'

'Can I call you Daddy?' Ben asked tentatively, and Phoebe's heart ached for him and for herself.

'Yes, certainly, Ben. There is nothing I would like better in the world than to have you call me Daddy,' Jed replied, and gave him a hug.

CHAPTER NINE

PHOEBE showered and dressed while Ben went with Jed for a swim in the indoor pool. She had only agreed to it after Jed had said they would walk down to the leisure centre and with a sardonic look had left her the keys to his car. He knew she did not trust him.

Emptying the cupboards, alone with her thoughts, Phoebe found her mind in turmoil. She feared for the future, Jed could give Ben anything money could buy, the rarefied lifestyle of the fabulously wealthy, and all she had to give her son was a working mother and lots of love… The odds seemed stacked against her. With a weary sigh she finished clearing the caravan. She could not help wondering if Ben would ever look on the simple pleasures they had shared here with the same enthusiasm after he was exposed to the more exotic people and places his father knew.

She tried not to let her misgivings show when the two returned, and if she was quiet then neither Ben nor Jed appeared to notice.

They spent the rest of the day driving from Weymouth to the start of Chesil Beach and the world heritage area of the Jurassic Coast—or, as Ben called it, the dinosaur coast. The beach ended at the town of Lyme Regis—a place that was renowned for the fossils to be found there. After a shy start and a few questions that Jed had answered simply Ben had with the innocence of youth accepted the man as his father, showing an ease and enthusiasm that made Phoebe feel guilty for keeping them apart for years and shamefully jealous. Ben was her son, and it was hard to accept she was no longer going to be the centre of his universe but would have to share that position with Jed.

Jed had enthralled Ben with his talk of family, and he was equally fascinated with Ben, searching for fossils on the beach. He actually found one—cracking open a rock with Ben's small hammer to find the outline of what looked like a dinosaur tooth, according to Ben.

Phoebe agreed. Jed had the luck of the devil and it made perfect sense to her.

When they returned to Peartree Cottage Sid met them at the door and after handing the keys to Phoebe left. Ben was over the moon at his newly decorated bedroom, and within half an hour he was bathed and fast asleep in bed.

'He looks angelic when he is asleep,' Jed murmured.

'Yes.'

Watching him staring down at Ben, seeing the gentle expression on his handsome face, softened Phoebe's heart. But it had hurt when Ben, his eyes gleaming with happiness, had kissed Jed and said, 'Goodnight, Daddy.'

'But he can be a devil sometimes—like his father,' she responded bitterly and, turning, she left the room and ran down the stairs.

She needed a coffee, and walked into the kitchen. She didn't know this creature she was turning into because of Jed—sharp-tongued and jealous at seeing her son kiss him and call him Daddy, confused and afraid of the future. Putting a spoonful of instant coffee in her 'Best Mum in the World' mug and pouring in boiling water, she smiled ruefully. When had she become so insecure she needed the comfort of an inanimate mug?

'I'll have a coffee, please, Phoebe.' Jed's rich dark voice cut into her thoughts and she had her answer.

'Okay,' she said, and prepared another mug with the instant brew, before turning around with a mug in each hand. He was standing much too close, watching her, and it had a disastrous effect on her nerves.

'Steady, Phoebe.' He took one mug from her not so steady hand and smiled—a breathtaking grin that deepened the laughter lines around his sparkling eyes and took years off his age. 'A very successful day—don't spoil it by covering me in hot coffee,' he joked, and, pulling out a chair, sat down at the kitchen table.

'Sit and enjoy your coffee,' he ordered. 'We have a lot to talk over.'

Successful for him, but not for her. She wanted to ignore him and his talk… Jed was much too dangerous to her life, to her emotional wellbeing, but she didn't really have a choice. Hear him out and see him out, she decided, and, stiff-backed, she pulled out a chair and sat opposite him at the kitchen table.

'So discuss—but make it fast. It has been a long day,' she said with heartfelt emphasis, 'and I am tired.'

'You look it,' he said, his dark eyes resting on her slender form perched at the end of the seat. He stretched out a hand and flipped the end of her long hair over her shoulder, brushing her neck as he did so.

She knew she looked a sight, but a day that had started with the emotional trauma of revealing Jed as Ben's father and continued with cleaning, packing and the rest of the time on a windswept beach would do that to any woman. Now the touch of his hand had made the hair on the back of her neck prickle and her body tingle—a state she had been in pretty much all weekend, much to her own self-disgust.

'Excuse me for not reaching your high standard of elegant designer-clad painted ladies, but then I never aspired to,' she said sarcastically.

Damn it to hell! Jed's mouth tightened. A tender gesture and a concerned comment on his part and she was bristling with outrage again. Patience and playing it cool was getting him nowhere. It was time she accepted the reality of the situation.

'Not for much longer,' he said bluntly. 'You soon will be the kind of elegantly clad lady you so abhor. Not for me—I could not give a damn what you wear, in fact naked works for me— But Ben deserves a mother who will blend easily into the society he will inevitably belong to, whether you like it or not. Tomorrow I have to be in London, but I will be back on Tuesday morning to pick you and Ben up. That gives you a day to pack. We should be at my home in Greece by the evening.'

Phoebe rose to her feet. She had listened in mounting resentment to his plan, and now she was furious at the stuck-up, arrogant devil trying to tell her what to do.

'No.' She gave him a filthy look. 'I am not going to Greece, and neither is Ben, until I decide the time is right. You have got your own way so far. Ben knows you are his father and you will have to be content with that. Now, you've finished your coffee and it is time you left.' Crossing the kitchen, she walked into the hall, shaking inside with anger.

Jed leapt to his feet and followed her. Grasping her elbow, he spun her around to face him. '*No* is not an answer I will accept. And your habit of running away is finished right now…understand?'

'I am *not* running away, and Ben and I are *not* going

anywhere with you on Tuesday or any time soon. You may order your minions around in your business life, but I will not let you do that with Ben and I. The answer is no...get over it.'

'You are being totally unreasonable. You have a week's holiday—there is nothing to stop you and Ben coming to Greece. You know he loves the seaside—I saw that this weekend—and even you have to admit spending every single holiday he has in a tiny caravan in Weymouth hardly compares to a holiday in Greece, with a much warmer climate, in a house overlooking the sea with every possible luxury,' he drawled sardonically. 'Ben would love it in Greece, and it is just your stubborn, pig-headed pride and distrust stopping him. Damn it, Phoebe, I can remember a time when you would have jumped at the chance. You had plans to travel and see the world. What the hell happened to you?'

For a long moment Phoebe stared at Jed, towering over her, conscious of his long fingers biting into her arm and the warmth of his great body. She could hear him breathing, he was that close, and she wished he would just go away and never come back. But fatalistically she knew it was not going to happen.

She had always known he was heartless, but his scathing comment about the caravan and his arrogance and total lack of sensitivity still had the power to shock and hurt her.

She had vowed never to let him hurt her again, and the simmering anger and resentment she had felt for years erupted. This was her life and she didn't have to justify her actions to any man—certainly not to Jed Sabbides, the egotistical male chauvinist before her.

She tilted back her head, her blue eyes blazing. '*You*

happened to me. You wrecked my life once and I will not allow you to do the same again.'

A chilling smile formed on his lips. 'What about Ben? Are you prepared to wreck *his* life because you are too much of a coward to face up to facts? You're a loving mother, I grant you, but he needs a man in his life because you are too soft with him.'

She flinched as though she had been struck, because his words touched a nerve—her Aunt Jemma had said much the same.

'Answer me this. Why did you allow me to take Ben out in the car on Friday night? Why did you allow me to spend not just the day but the whole weekend with you both?'

'Because you were like a flaming juggernaut, flattening every objection I made,' she flung at him, hating to think he might be right.

'Flattered though I am to think I have that much influence over you, the truth is it is *Ben* who has that much influence over you. I have watched and listened, and you are so reluctant to upset the boy you allow him to get his own way—and he knows it, Phoebe. Trust me, I am his father—and I was the same with my mother until my father taught me different.' He gave her a dry smile. 'While it is not a problem now, it will be in the future without a strong male influence to guide him. You let him pressure you into telling him I was his father before you could get out of bed this morning, and yesterday you let him have two different wall coverings—which I could tell you didn't want—rather than telling him to make a decision. Something he will have to learn to do if he is to succeed in life.'

Phoebe was badly shaken by his assessment of her parenting skills, because deep down she had a horrible feeling there was some truth in what he said. But she wasn't about to let him see how she felt.

'Who made *you* a child psychologist?' she jeered. 'For a man who never had a child on his agenda, and has known he was a father for all of three days, you have some nerve commenting on my parenting skills. If you think by manipulating Ben he will persuade me to go to Greece forget it… That is the worst type of parenting, but typical of a ruthless swine like you,' she flashed back.

His smile vanished. He looked at her with a rage that made every nerve in her body jump. 'You little—' He began, and then broke off, his arm encircling her waist to pull her roughly against him.

There was a long fraught silence, and Phoebe was not quite sure what was going to happen next. She knew only that they were locked together, and she was helplessly aware of the hard planes and angles of his body against her much softer frame. When his other hand stroked over her shoulder to curve around the nape of her neck her whole body trembled.

Jed felt the tension in her, felt her tremble, and some of his rage faded. 'Don't flatter yourself. Persuading you to come to Greece is not my main objective, but the boy is,' he told her bluntly. 'We both know you fell into my arms the other night all ready and willing, and you would do the same again right now.'

Her eyes were enormous, the pupils darkening as he watched, and deliberately he tightened his hold, easing a leg between her thighs and stroking a hand down over the soft wool of her sweater, settling on the proud swell of her breast.

'You can fling out that old accusation of me not wanting a child, Phoebe,' he murmured against her ear, lightly biting on the small lobe, and he heard the audible intake of her breath as he added, 'And of wanting you to have a termination. You can keep telling yourself you still believe

such a crazy idea, but the only person you are fooling is
yourself.'

'Says you,' she murmured—but it was a weak defence,
and Jed saw the flush of arousal in her cheeks. God! She
was so beautiful, so sensual, and so damn stubborn. And
he was as hard as a rock and almost groaned.

It irritated the hell out of him that from the moment he
saw her he wanted her, with a consuming hunger that defied
all logic, and an absence of years had made no difference.
It annoyed him too that he who had always prided himself
on his ability to control every aspect of his life struggled
to control his passion with Phoebe.

Reigning in his raging libido, he eased her slightly away
from him before he lost it completely and took her where
they stood.

'I am not arguing with you any more, Phoebe, and nor
am I taking you to bed to ease the ache you quite clearly
have.' Dropping his hand from her waist, he moved back
and surveyed her from beneath heavy-lidded eyes. 'I have
wasted enough time in the past few weeks tracking you
down. I can't force you to come with me, but I *will* be back
on Tuesday, about noon, to pick you both up, and you *will*
spend at least the rest of the week in Greece.'

'You expect me to agree just like that?' Phoebe demanded. He had only to take her in his arms and every
sensible thought flew out of her brain, but now, no longer
overwhelmed by the warmth of his body, his soft caresses,
his comment about *wasting time tracking her down* had
cooled her ardor and she finally found her voice. 'Well,
dream on—because I won't.'

A slow smile formed on his lips. 'Stubbornness is an
unbecoming trait in a beautiful woman.' His dark eyes,
glittering with blatant sensuality, captured hers. 'Think it
over, hmm?'

'I don't need to think,' she spat, her anger rising to eclipse any vestige of sensual awareness. 'I don't want to.' She saw the narrowing of his eyes and added, 'Well, not yet.' Her common sense was telling her she could not afford to antagonise Jed completely. 'Custody arrangements take time to be arranged legally to suit all parties. You can't just order people around.'

'As you please,' Jed drawled, low and lethal. 'Then I will see you in court.'

The colour drained from her face. 'Court? You want to go to court?'

'As you seem incapable of coming to a private agreement, I don't see any other solution.' Her blue eyes widened fearfully as with one finger Jed pushed up her chin, and she stared up at his hard face. 'The decision is yours. You have a day to decide.'

His dark head dipped, and before she registered what he intended his mouth had covered hers in a hard, possessive kiss that in a second had her lips parting helplessly beneath his. With a will of their own her slender arms slid up around his broad shoulders, her fingers digging into the wool of his sweater, and she swayed into the heat of his great body, the heavy thudding of her heart deafening her to everything but the exquisite taste and touch of Jed.

Suddenly he broke the kiss and, straightening up, took her hands from his shoulders and pushed her gently away from him.

'I'd better leave now.'

In an oddly tender gesture he lifted a finger and tucked a few stray tendrils of hair behind her ear. For a moment she was completely disorientated, still under the magical spell of his kiss—until her eyes focused on his face and saw the mocking amusement in his smile.

'Otherwise I might be tempted to stay again.' His finger

fell from her face. 'You want me—you can't help yourself, Phoebe—but the next time I make love to you will be *after* Ben's future is successfully decided, not before.' He turned to go and then glanced back. 'By the way, I forgot to use protection the other night—so I trust you are better at taking the contraceptive pill than you were in the past.' His dark eyes met hers 'It won't be a problem, I hope?'

'Of course not,' she responded, and he simply nodded his head and left.

But his exit line had been a killer...

How long Phoebe stood looking vacantly into space, her heart pounding in her chest, she had no idea. Finally she staggered into the living room and flopped down on the sofa, her mind spinning.

She had not taken the contraceptive pill since she and Jed had split up—but no way was she admitting the fact. Frantically she did the calculations and sighed. It was a week before her period—not too bad.

Plus, last time they had been in Paris and they'd had sex dozens of times. Once on the sofa didn't pack the same punch. She hit the sofa, as though the furniture was at fault.

If it was anyone's fault it was Jed's. He never forgot protection. At the beginning of their affair he had been meticulous in his use of condoms until he was certain the birth control pill had had time to take full effect. In fact she would not put it past the man to have deliberately 'forgotten' to use protection the other night.

She was being unrealistic, she knew. If she was pregnant—and it was a huge if—she had no one to blame but herself. As well as history she actually taught the sex education classes at school...how ironic was that?

To be fair to Jed, it was natural for him to expect her to be on the pill, given her age and past experience...

Especially as she had told him she saw sex as a pleasure between consenting rather than committed adults now, and had let him believe she was more than a friend to Julian...

Wearily she pulled the band from her hair. She could feel the beginnings of a headache coming on and, closing her eyes, she ran her hands through her hair. Actually, she was pretty near tearing it out in frustration at her own stupidity.

She opened her eyes and rose to her feet. There was no point sitting here fearing the worst. She might as well go to bed...

But would being pregnant be the worst thing in the world? she mused lying in bed half an hour later, praying for the oblivion of sleep. Ben would be delighted to have a brother or sister—being an only child herself, she knew it could be lonely. Under normal circumstances, secure in a loving marriage, she would have liked two or three children. But her circumstances were not normal, and never could be with Jed Sabbides...

Her weakness for Jed's body did not cloud her mind to the sort of man he really was. He didn't do love—he had told her so quite emphatically on one unforgettable occasion. He might possibly feel love for a child—she could not deny he was great with Ben—but heaven help any woman he married, because without love she was pretty certain he wouldn't do fidelity either...

Getting Ben his breakfast the next morning, she mentioned to him the possibility of going to Greece for a holiday some time and he was all for it. But Phoebe was still not convinced, still undecided...

The day got worse when she and Ben walked down to the village, where he told everyone they met he had a daddy. Not that it was necessary. The hospital receptionist and the local grapevine had already done their work well, and when she walked into the post office the postmistress asked her when the wedding was.

CHAPTER TEN

As it happened, in the end Phoebe did not have to make the decision as it was made for her...

She gave up trying to sleep at six the next morning, and got out of bed and checked on Ben. He was still asleep—probably because she had let him stay up late last night. She had not wanted to be alone with her thoughts.

Not that it had done her much good. She was no nearer reaching a decision even as she took a long shower. She lathered the soap down over her body and slowly back up to her throat, then raked her fingers through her long hair. She tilted her head back and felt the warm jets pound against her overheated flesh, and a vivid image of Jed nuzzling her breasts filled her mind. With a low groan she grasped the bottle of shampoo and washed her hair with more vigour than necessary. Then, turning the water to cold, she stood under the freezing spray.

When she was sure the heat and the sensual hunger that had invaded her body since the reappearance of Jed Sabbides in her life was finally extinguished, she turned off the water and stepped out of the shower.

Damn! She could hear the distant ring of the telephone. Snatching a bathtowel from the cupboard, she wrapped it around her shivering body and rushed downstairs, wondering who on earth could be calling this early.

Phoebe picked up the receiver, and before she could utter a word Jed's deep dark voice resonated in her ear.

'Where the hell have you been? I have been trying to call you for twenty minutes.'

'I was in the shower, and now I am standing shivering in the hall with only a towel for warmth, so—'

He cut her off. 'Hell and damnation, Phoebe! I need a picture of you near naked in my mind like a hole in the head right now,' he growled in a deep frustrated tone, and the calming effect of her cold shower disappeared.

'Just be quiet and listen. My father had a heart attack last night. He is in hospital, in Intensive Care, and I arrived in Greece at three this morning.'

'I'm so sorry,' Phoebe said, her heart touched. Even Jed, hard as he was, had to feel bad when it came to his father's health.

'I don't want your sympathy. I just want you to do as I say. I've spoken to his consultant and the next forty-eight hours are crucial. He is in and out of consciousness, but I have told him about Ben and he wants to meet him. There is no way I am going to let my father die without seeing his grandson. A car will be arriving at your door at nine, to take you both to the airport. I've arranged for Sid to accompany you, and he will bring you to the hospital—understand?'

'Yes—no. Wait,' she stammered, her heart no longer aching with sympathy but racing in panic.

'I have no time to argue. Just do as I say.' And he hung up.

Phoebe took Ben's hand in hers and gave him a reassuring smile as they walked down the hospital corridor to Intensive Care. 'You will see Daddy soon, and you are going to meet your grandfather, who is not very well. But don't be afraid—he will be fine.'

'Sid said I'm a big boy and not afraid of anything,' Ben said. 'Isn't that right, Sid?'

'Sure thing.' Sid smiled at Phoebe over the top of his head. 'Don't worry—take a seat.' He indicated the chairs against one wall. 'I'll tell Mr Sabbides you are here.' And he walked through the door opposite.

Phoebe watched the door swing closed and sank gratefully down on a chair, urging Ben to sit down beside her. She was scared. Events had moved so fast she felt as if she had lost all control, and it terrified her.

After Jed had called she had woken Ben up and told him they were going to Greece in a plane to see his daddy. He'd been thrilled. Reluctantly she had packed a few things, knowing she could not ignore the wishes of a dying man.

That was if the man *was* dying! She would not put it past Jed to use his father to get his own way. He'd had no trouble in using Ben over the daddy issue on Sunday, she had reminded herself, and she'd still not been certain about their going. But when a grim-faced Sid had arrived on her doorstep and confirmed the facts she'd locked up the house and got into the car.

Phoebe glanced around. It was hard to believe that after answering the telephone at home that morning she was now sitting in a hospital corridor in Athens this afternoon, not knowing what to expect next.

Suddenly the door opposite swung open and Sid walked out. 'Mr Sabbides will be here in a second, so I'll leave you now,' he said, and left.

Warily Phoebe watched the still swinging door, her nerves knotting painfully in the pit of her stomach as Jed appeared.

'Phoebe—you came,' he said, in an unfamiliar hoarse tone.

She looked up at his grim face 'Yes.' Their eyes held

for tense, interminable seconds, the shadows of their past intimacy melding with the present to create a rare moment of mutual understanding.

'I wasn't sure you would,' he admitted. 'But I am glad you did.'

Phoebe tore her eyes from his and let her gaze sweep over him. He had shed the jacket of his suit somewhere, and his pants were crumpled. The open-necked shirt he wore was equally crumpled. His dark hair lay in dishevelled strands across his forehead, as if he had combed his fingers through it countless times, and his heavy-lidded eyes were strained in a face that looked oddly grey.

Concern for him flooded over her, and she had an impulsive desire to leap to her feet and take him in her arms. But she fought to control the impulse, determined not to let him see it.

'You did not give me a lot of choice,' she rebuked, mildly but softened it with a faint smile. Now was not the time to argue. 'As for Ben—he couldn't get on the plane fast enough. He has never flown before, and was totally fascinated.'

'I'm going to be a pilot when I grow up, Daddy,' Ben said.

The glimmer of a smile curved the tight line of Jed's mouth as he bent down and swept Ben up into his arms. 'You can be anything you like when you grow up, but right now I want you to meet your grandfather.' And, glancing at Phoebe, he added, 'My father wants to see you as well, Phoebe. The doctor has given him something and he is awake at the moment, but for how long...' He shrugged his broad shoulders. 'Come,' he said, and, rising to her feet, she followed Jed and Ben into the other room.

A small dark-haired woman walked towards her. 'I am Jed's sister Cora,' she said, and with a smile and a hello for

Ben she looked up at Phoebe. 'You must be Phoebe. I have heard so much about you, and it is lovely to finally meet you, but I wish it was in happier circumstances. You must come to dinner tonight and meet the rest of the family.'

'No, not tonight,' Jed cut in, putting Ben down on his feet. 'You go and get a coffee or something. We won't be long here, and then you can take over for a few hours while I take Phoebe and Ben home.'

With a roll of her huge dark eyes his sister murmured, 'The oracle has spoken,' and put her hand on Phoebe's arm. 'I love my brother, but I know him. Don't let him bully you. I'll bring the children over tomorrow morning—they will be company for Ben. Whatever Jed thinks, a sickroom is no place for young children,' she said with a sad smile. 'I'll see you later.'

Phoebe smiled back, feeling marginally better. Cora seemed friendly, though her comment about having heard a lot about her had been odd, she thought as Cora left the room. Then, taking a deep steadying breath, she turned and froze as she took in the tableau before her.

A white-haired man lay on the bed, his head propped up by pillows, a discarded oxygen mask around his neck, and lines attached to his wrist and chest leading to a drip. A bank of monitors was recording all his vital functions. His face was lined with age and pain, but there was no mistaking his distinctive features.

Ben, who was just big enough to see over the bed, was looking curiously at his grandfather as Jed said something in Greek to his father, and then switched to English to introduce Ben.

She saw the old man's dull eyes light up with such joy it brought a lump to her throat, and she saw Ben hold out his hand and the old man take it. She was looking at three generations of a family—all male, all with the same deep brown eyes, all smiling, all with the same thick slightly curling hair. They looked incredibly alike—no one could ever mistake them for anything other than family. Suddenly it hit Phoebe like a punch in the stomach. Ben fitted in seamlessly with these men. This was his family, however much she wished it wasn't, and she had no right to deny him the benefits of his paternal family.

'You are a very old man,' she heard Ben say.

'Really, Ben—it is bad manners to make personal comments.' But her admonishment was drowned by Jed's laugh and his father's chuckle.

'The truth does not hurt,' Jed's father said in a weak rasping voice. 'Come closer, where I can see you.'

Phoebe moved to stand by Ben and Jed, and glanced warily down at the bed's occupant, not quite sure what to expect.

'You are the mother of my wonderful grandson,' he said, eyes glistening with moisture meeting hers. 'I thank you with my heart so very much for bringing him to me.'

'My pleasure,' Phoebe murmured. 'I am pleased to meet you,' she continued rather formally, 'and I hope you recover soon.' She did not trust herself to say any more, and swallowed down the emotion welling up inside her. His English was heavily accented, and nowhere near as fluent as Jed's, and she could tell he was struggling to breathe, but there was no mistaking the genuine delight and the wealth of emotion in his tone.

His gaze swept slowly over her, and then he looked at Jed and spoke in Greek for a couple of minutes while she watched. She was amazed to see a dark flush spread over Jed's high cheekbones, and he actually looked embarrassed when he finally responded.

Then his father turned his eyes on Phoebe, a determined gleam in the dark depths. 'You are beautiful, Phoebe.'

He grasped her hand with a strength she would not have thought possible in his condition. 'My son is an idiot. You must excuse him. His mother and I taught him better. He will marry you immediately, and I—'

'Enough Father! This is not the time,' Jed commanded, and she saw him glance and frown at the bank of monitors before looking back at his father. 'These things can wait. You must rest.'

'You have waited too long already,' his father sighed, letting go of Phoebe's hand as he sank deeper into the pillows. The small burst of strength he seemed to have had was fading as his eyes closed. 'I no longer have time, and you would not deny an old man's last wish to see you wed.'

Talk about emotional blackmail! The old man was a master. That was Phoebe's first thought, but watching Jed lean forward to place the oxygen mask on his father's face, murmuring something in his own language and then pressing a kiss on the lined brow before straightening up, she suddenly felt terribly guilty for her unkind thought. The old man really was fighting for his life… But what made warmth flow through her and moisture haze her eyes was seeing the hard, emotionless Jed she had tried for so long to hate carefully tending to his father.

'He is asleep.' Jed smiled down at Ben and, taking the boy's hand, glanced at Phoebe. 'Cora is going to sit with him. We can go now.'

He looped an arm around her shoulder and ushered them out of the room. To any onlooker she realised they must look like a real family—and would it really be so bad if they were? Shocked at where her thoughts were leading, she stiffened—and was suddenly conscious of the subtle brush of Jed's long leg against her thigh as he ushered them along the corridor.

Self-disgust at the ease with which he could affect her physically—in a hospital of all places!—mingled with the confusion and resentment she felt towards Jed. He knew her too well in some respects. In the past he had told her often enough she was too soft-hearted for her own good with her friends, beggars and stray animals… It was all his fault she was in this almost helpless position in a foreign country.

She shrugged his hand from her shoulder and turned to look at him.

'Not now, Phoebe. Recriminations can wait,' he said, accurately reading her mind. 'I have had a hell of a night and the day isn't getting any better. As for my father…' He shook his head. 'Damn him—he is unbelievable.'

She glanced at him in surprise 'That isn't a very nice thing to say.'

'Phoebe, all I want to do is get you two home and have a shower and a change of clothes.' He closed his eyes and pinched the bridge of his nose with his fingers, then opened them again. 'Maybe an hour's sleep.'

She looked at him—really looked at him—and realised with a sense of shock that Jed the dynamic, powerful man she had thought indefatigable actually looked almost exhausted…

'You look like you could use it,' she responded as they left the building.

Jed dropped into the front passenger seat of the car and let his head fall back against the rest. His son and Phoebe were here, and he felt relief flow through him. His father had met Ben and the old man was content. But the anger he felt because it had taken his father's near death to bring about the meeting simmered inside him. Whatever the outcome of the next forty-eight hours—no thirty hours now—his father's lifespan would be drastically reduced.

Weary though he was, the knowledge that Phoebe had kept his son's existence from him for years was never far from his mind. *He* still had plenty of time to get to know his son, but his father probably did not.

Thinking of his father's last order, he pulled out his cellphone and called his lawyer. He had to admire the old man—he was not done yet.

The house was some way out of the city on the coast, and stood in acres of grounds—a veritable mansion, with panoramic views of the sea. Ben was awestruck, as was Phoebe when Jed led them into a huge hall. A worried-looking woman appeared and Jed introduced them both to the housekeeper, Maria, who luckily spoke a little English and then spoke rapidly in Greek to Jed, while Phoebe glanced interestedly around.

An extravagant curving staircase was the centrepiece of the huge marble-floored reception hall, which had at least half a dozen rooms leading off. Suddenly one of the doors opened and a woman appeared… Sophia! Phoebe recognised her immediately as she dashed past her to grab Jed's arm, her dark eyes fixed on his as she spoke hurriedly in Greek.

Phoebe stood like a block of wood, her eyes darting from one to the other in amazement. That they were intimate friends was obvious by the way Sophia held Jed's arm and then placed her other hand on his chest. But then she had always known that—so why did she feel so sick inside at the sight of the pair of them together, and so betrayed all over again…?

Because she still loved Jed… The unwanted thought popped into her head. No. She could not—would not—succumb again to something that had hurt her so dreadfully in the past. She doubted she had the strength to survive it again. One night of sex and a weekend together had left her aching for more, but it was lust, not love. Probably seeing a tender side of Jed with Ben and his father was addling her brain, she told herself, and took a step back—both figuratively and mentally.

She reminded herself that only a few days ago Sophia had been a woman supposedly no longer speaking to him, according to Jed—the low-life rat… The woman who was now in his home and rattling away in Greek. The woman he was gently clasping by the shoulders and easing away from him with a smile…

'Thank you for your concern, Sophia, but I'm sure my father will be fine. Speak English, please—I have guests.' Propelling Ben forward with one hand, he said, 'My son Benjamin.' As an afterthought he added, 'His mother Phoebe you have met.'

'Your son!' Sophia exclaimed, but quickly recovered and said, 'Hello, Benjamin,' before turning to look at her. 'Of course I remember you, Phoebe,' Sophia said. 'How could I forget?' She gave a polite smile that did not reach her eyes, and then looked down at Ben again, then back to her, and frowned. 'Though I seem to recall you did not remember Jed at the time—and now you are in his house with your child. How bizarre.' And she spoke to Jed again in her own language.

Phoebe saw Jed stiffen as he replied, and saw the flash of some emotion in Sophia's eyes. A moment later she shook her head, a wry smile on her scarlet lips.

Then Jed reverted to English. 'Thank your father for his concern, but now you will have to excuse us, Sophia—it has been a long day. Maria will show you out.'

Sophia gave Phoebe a curious glance. 'The boy is undeniably the image of his father. I can't decide if you are a fool or very clever.' She shrugged her shoulders. 'Either way I wish you luck. You are going to need it with Jed, believe me.' Then with a careless wave of her hand in farewell she followed Maria to the door.

In a way Phoebe almost felt sorry for Sophia. She had come closer than any other female to marrying the most eligible bachelor in Greece... At the ambassador's ball her father had hinted as much to Phoebe and Julian while the couple was on the dance floor. So what had gone wrong? she wondered. Maybe nothing had, she thought cynically.

'The news of my father's heart attack was on the local radio,' Jed explained, and reached for her arm. She shrugged him off.

'For someone who is not speaking to you, Sophia was amazingly loquacious,' Phoebe said sarcastically.

'She was here to offer her family's support to my father in any way she could—a natural response from friends.'

'An extremely good friend, you lying toad...'

His eyes narrowed and his expression became darkly forbidding. As Maria approached he said to Ben, 'Go with Maria, son—she will give you a drink.'

Phoebe opened her mouth to object, but Ben was happy to do as his daddy said, and walked away with the housekeeper.

'You will *never* call me a liar in front of Ben again,' Jed commanded harshly. 'He does not need to hear your derogatory comments and jealous grumbles.'

'Jealous of you? Don't make me laugh.' But he was closer to the truth than Phoebe cared to admit, and on the premise that attack was the best form of defense she struck back. 'Unlike you, I am not in the habit of lying. Do you actually think I *want* to be here with you? Well, I don't. The only reason I am here is for Ben and your father's sake. Unlike you, I have a heart and would never, ever turn down a seriously ill old man's request—that would be unconscionable.'

'Good,' he said, an arrested expression on his face. 'You have no idea how glad I am to hear that,' he added with a chuckle. 'Now, if you will excuse me, I need a shower. Maria will show you around.' And in a few lithe strides he crossed the foyer and ascended the stairs.

Phoebe, her mouth tightening into a grim line, saw nothing amusing in what she had said—quite the opposite. The past few days had been sheer hell, and things did not look like improving any time soon. She sighed, and was relieved to see Ben running towards her with Maria a few steps behind.

'Mum, I have had cake made of honey and stuff.'

Maria laughed and wiped his mouth with a tissue. 'The boy is so quick.' She beamed. 'But now I show you around the house, yes?'

Phoebe agreed, and was suitably impressed—over-awed would be nearer the mark, she thought, after wandering in and out of five reception rooms, some formal and some not, a study and a garden room. The basement contained a gym and a great swimming pool, and the upstairs was equally impressive.

Maria told her there were two bedroom suites plus a further five bedrooms, all *en-suite*, and on the top floor were the staff quarters. Finally she showed Phoebe into two adjoining rooms for her and Ben, and suggested that after their long journey they might like to get washed and settled and then maybe have something to eat. Dinner was usually at nine, but with the master in hospital it was any time anyone was home. She showed Phoebe how to use the in-house telephone, and told her to give her a call when they were ready to eat.

An hour later, washed and changed and sitting at the

table in the surprisingly homely breakfast room, with Ben making short work of scrambled eggs and grilled tomatoes Phoebe smiled indulgently. He loved anything red—including his food. She forked the last mouthful of egg into her mouth and sat back, feeling almost relaxed—until Jed walked in.

Involuntarily Phoebe stiffened in the chair. Jed's hair was slicked back, still damp from the shower. He'd shaved and dressed in a dark pinstriped suit, white shirt and sombre tie, but he no longer looked so tired. In fact he looked gorgeous, and she stared helplessly at him, trying to still her racing pulse but frighteningly conscious of the superb powerful male physique beneath the conservative attire. She fought to resist the effect of his potent masculinity on her vulnerable senses so much that it hurt to tear her gaze away.

She had tried to tell herself she was over him and despised him—had done for years. But since he had seduced her the other night, with a tender passion that had cut through her every defense with humiliating ease, she was forced to admit she was lying to herself. She would never be over Jed. It was as if her body was wired only to respond to his, and she doubted she would ever meet another man to take his place…

Jed strolled forward, his dark gaze skimming over Phoebe. She had changed into a dress that clung to her full firm breasts. Trying to ignore the gnawing frustration he felt, he lifted his eyes to her face. In the bright light of the room she looked pale, and he saw the flickering shadows in the wary blue eyes that met his. He sensed tension and something more as she clasped her hands in her lap and looked down.

For a moment his conscience worried him, and then he looked at Ben.

'I thought I'd find you here, Ben.' He pushed aside any niggling doubt at his tactics. Phoebe had deceived him five years ago, and again at the embassy ball. She didn't deserve any sympathy—not from him. 'I have to go out, son.' He glanced at his watch. 'And as I will not be back before your bedtime I'll say goodnight now. Sleep well.'

He ruffled the dark hair, and with a nod to Phoebe he left.

CHAPTER ELEVEN

PHOEBE walked down the grand staircase. The house was quiet—eerily so. Ben was fast asleep—she had checked on him twice already. She glanced at her wristwatch. Ten-thirty, but she was too on edge to go to bed. She remembered seeing a television in the family room downstairs—surely there must be some channel she could watch? Trouble was she could not remember exactly which door it was. She opened one—the dining room—and closed it, then moved to the next one and opened it. A window lamp was the only illumination and she stepped inside, her eyes adjusting to the dim light, and realised it was the study.

'Come in and join me in a drink,' a deep voice slurred, and she saw Jed sprawled on a large black leather sofa, a glass in his hand. 'I could use the company.'

'No. I'll… Are you all right?' she asked, concerned that he sounded drunk,

'I don't know. Tomorrow will tell.'

Phoebe felt dreadful. She had been so concerned with her own worries, protecting her own feelings, she had never considered how worried Jed must be, given the first forty-eight hours were crucial to his father's recovery and half of that time had already gone. He had said *Damn the man* when they'd left the hospital, but she had seen the gentle way he cared for him, and had realized Jed was not the emotionless zombie she had thought—at least not where his father was concerned. Maybe he was too emotionally repressed to tell his father how he felt.

Her tender heart went out to him, and tentatively she moved towards him. 'I did not know you were back,' she murmured, stopping in front of him. His pin-striped jacket was draped on the arm of the sofa, he had pulled his tie free, and his shirt lay open at the neck, revealing the strong line of his throat. He was all arrogant, sexy male—and yet he looked so alone...

She sat down beside him. 'Jed?' He lifted his head to look at her. 'I know how you feel, but drinking will not help you.'

'You could not possibly know how I feel,' he said, draining the glass of whisky in his hand. Placing the glass on the side table, he lounged back on the sofa.

'But I do.' She laid a consoling hand on his forearm. 'When my parents had the car accident my mother died instantly, and I never got the chance to tell her I loved her. But my father lived for a week, and though it was heart-wrenching to see him fading it gave me the chance to tell him how much I appreciated him and loved him, and to say goodbye. With luck your father might have years left, but if not he is still here now. I know you care for him, so instead of damning him you should tell him you love him. Trust me—it will make you feel a whole lot better.'

'Ah, Phoebe!' Jed drawled softly, and slid his arm around her shoulders to draw her close. She was so soft-hearted, so typically female—all for revealing emotions. He almost felt sorry for what he was about to do.

'I'm grateful for your concern, but it is not necessary.' Her big blue eyes were staring up at him, and he reached and ran a finger down the her cheek, letting his hand rest on her breastbone. He saw her catch her breath and fought the temptation to cover her mouth with his own and take what he knew was his to take. But he had done that on Friday and it had sent her running. He could not take the chance. Everything was in place, and time was of the essence. He could wait another day...

'My damning comment was an expression of admiration for my father, not a condemnation,' he continued. 'He knows exactly how I feel about him. We made up any differences we had after he divorced his fourth wife. He explained to me why he'd married so often—it was because he loved my mother, worshipped and adored her. She was his soul mate. But when she knew she was terminally ill she made him promise he would marry again, and not become the kind of man who had no respect for woman and slept around. Probably because that was what he was like before he met her,' he said dryly. 'My father kept the promise, the silly old fool, and the only women he has had sex with since her death he has married.'

This was a Jed Phoebe had never heard before, confiding intimate details about his family. 'That is not silly but quite romantic—keeping his promise. He must be a wonderful old man,' Phoebe said. 'Not a cynic like you.' She dared to tease him.

'Romantic, yes. The jury is still out on cynic,' Jed drawled, and tightened his arm over her shoulder in case she tried to bolt. 'But will you still think he is a wonderful old man tomorrow, when we get married?'

'*What?*' Phoebe spluttered, lifting her stunned gaze to his. He had to be joking... His dark eyes stared back, humourless and hard, and there was a determination about his handsome features that told her he was not.

'You heard, Phoebe... My father wants to see us married—he told you so—and he told me to arrange the ceremony while you were standing there. I agreed in order to placate him. If it makes it easier for you, I never had sex with Sophia. We have been friends for years, and I considered marrying her because our fathers are great friends. It seemed sensible—a marriage of convenience much the same as we will have.'

The fact he had never slept with Sophia pleased her, though she was loath to admit it. As for the rest—his emotionless approach to a marriage to placate his father enraged her.

'You agreed? Are you out of your mind?'

'No. I simply took you at your word this afternoon when you said you *did not lie* and unlike me *you had a heart* and would *never, ever turn down a seriously ill old man's request* because that would be *unconscionable*. So, Phoebe, my father has requested we marry… Are you a woman of your word?' Jed looked at her, his smile filled with arrogant amusement. 'Or, like most females, are you going to try and wriggle out of it?'

She felt as if she had been doused in a bucket of cold water. All her tender feelings vanished. She *had* said all that, and meant it, but it had never entered her head that Jed would try and use her emotional outburst to suit himself. She should have remembered Jed was a man who always got what he wanted. He had lulled her into a false sense of security and then dropped his bombshell.

She tilted her head back, the light of battle in her gaze. 'That is the most disingenuous take on what I said. Only you would have the gall to come up with it.'

'No worse than you turning my offer to take care of you when you were pregnant into a demand for termination, or denying me and my father precious years with Ben,' he said grimly. 'Now you can make some recompense. The wedding is arranged for tomorrow at the hospital. All you have to do is turn up and sign when you're told.'

'I'm not a fool,' she tossed back. 'It is impossible. You cannot get married that fast. You need documents—birth certificates.'

His hand moved from her chest to curve around her neck. 'All taken care of. Sid gave me your passports, and when I left earlier it was to meet with the Mayor—a friend of my father's— He granted us a special dispensation, owing to my father's precarious state of health, for a civil marriage service to take place tomorrow by his bedside.'

'You stole my passport.' She had handed them to Sid when they had come through passport control at the airport and forgotten to ask for them back.

'No—borrowed it.' He tipped back her head and looked at her mouth, and then down her long, elegant throat to where the creamy curve of her breasts was exposed by the dipping neckline of her dress, and then back to her face. 'We had some good times the year we were together. We could again. Would it be so hard to be married to me, Phoebe?' he asked, bringing his mouth down on hers as she opened her mouth to answer.

He expertly took advantage of her parted lips to ease his tongue between them and sensually explore the moist interior of her mouth. She told herself it wasn't what she wanted, but he kissed her with an ever deepening passion that proved her a liar as, boneless, she leant against him and kissed him back.

When he finally released her he was breathing hard. It gave her some comfort to know he was equally affected by the passion they shared—until he spoke.

'You know marriage makes sense. Ben will be happy, my father will be happy, and we have this intense physical connection. What could be better?' he prompted, a glint of satisfaction in his sensual smile.

'What about love?' she had to ask.

'Love is simply another word for lust. Try to think logically, Phoebe. A man will live contentedly in a marriage if the sex is good. No sex, but just the emotion you call love, and he will not be content for long and will look for sex elsewhere.'

Phoebe stiffened, squaring her shoulders. 'That is the most cynical statement I have ever heard.' She looked at him with angry eyes. The condescending swine, with his *try to be logical*, and his callous dismissal of love. The whole focus of his life was power and money. This way he got a child to leave it to and to carry on his flaming name, with a bit of recreational sex with a convenient wife thrown in.

She wanted to smack the self-satisfied smile off his handsome face but she thought of Ben and hesitated. Then there was the chance she might be pregnant. It was not very likely, but the way her luck was running lately it was a possibility. Two illegitimate children was too many. Glancing up through the thick fringe of her lashes, she could not deny Jed was a wickedly attractive and virile man, lounging back with his hands resting lightly on his thighs. Once she had loved him with all her heart, but not any more. Well, to hell with him—she would play him at his own game.

'Yes, I will marry you,' she agreed.

But little did he know sex was out… Let the arrogant devil try living without and see how long he lasted before she could divorce him for adultery…

'Thank you.' He dropped a patronising kiss on the top of her head. 'I knew you would see sense.'

'You are right as usual,' she said, and the sarcasm in her tone was lost on him.

'I'm glad we finally agree,' he said, and stood up. He turned to pick his jacket up, then shrugged it on. 'I have to go to the hospital so Cora can get home.' He glanced back down at her. 'I will tell her and my father the good news. She was coming here in the morning with her family anyway, so she can help you find something to wear.' He flicked a finger under her chin 'Relax—don't worry. Everything will be fine.' And he left.

Phoebe stood still as a statue at Jed's side, by his father's hospital bed. The old man was propped up on pillows, his face flushed and his eyes glittering—whether it was a good sign or not, she didn't know. She glanced around. The whole set-up was surreal. Heart monitors bleeping away, an official on the other side of the bed talking. She had not a clue what he was saying.

Mercifully, the civil ceremony was brief. Cora and her husband Theo were the witnesses—and surprisingly Dr Marcus. She watched numbly as Jed signed the necessary documents, and took the pen from his long fingers and signed where he indicated. It was all over with a complete lack of ceremony or emotion. Except for the moment when Jed took her in his arms and kissed her. Then the numbness cleared and she looked dazedly up at him, her heart pounding, until the pop of a champagne cork restored her senses.

Glasses were filled and handed around; a toast was made to the bride and groom. Cora helped her father to one sip, and then the consultant ordered them all out.

Phoebe glanced up at the man who was now her husband as he cupped her elbow in his palm and ushered her out into the corridor. He looked as cool and controlled as ever, dressed in a perfectly tailored grey suit, and looking as if he had concluded yet another successful business deal.

A reception room in the private hospital had been set aside for the wedding party, and she blinked as Jed led her in and twenty or more people gathered around. Jed introduced her, but she was too numb with nerves to take in their names because her confidence in her ability to hold to the line of the no-sex marriage she had envisaged had faded somewhat with her temper...and Jed's kiss.

Champagne corks popped, speeches were made, toasts drunk, and Jed finally left her side to speak to some people. She was glad to be alone for a moment.

But not for long. Dr Marcus cornered her, a champagne glass in his hand, looking slightly tipsy.

'Phoebe, dear!' he exclaimed. 'You look wonderful. I was so pleased to hear of your miracle child, and now this.' He flung his arm wildly to encompass the room. 'It has been a long time coming, but Jed has finally persuaded you to marry him and I am delighted for you both. I remember the awful night you were taken to hospital. Jed and I had had dinner together earlier. He buries his emotions deep but I could tell he was thrilled about the baby, and he told me he was going to marry you. He dropped me off first, and of course when he got home tragedy struck.' He took a sip champagne and Phoebe went pale at his revelations. Marcus had no reason to lie.

'Jed was devastated when he got to the hospital and heard the news, poor man—and for a long time afterwards. It didn't help that the same weekend his father had his first massive heat attack—the day after his birthday. He was in this same hospital, in Intensive Care as he is now, with Jed at his side for forty-eight hours. Jed thought he had lost you when he finally got back to London, but fate moves in mysterious ways. He has found you again and married you at last. It was always meant to be. Fate cannot be denied for long,' he declared expansively, 'and I know you will both be incredibly happy.'

One shock followed another: from hearing Jed had been going to marry her to realising Jed had not deliberately deserted her. Before she could formulate a response for the smiling Marcus, Jed appeared and put an arm around her waist.

'What are you saying to my wife, Marcus?' he demanded of his friend.

'Congratulating her, of course.'

'Are you all right?' Jed murmured as Marcus was hailed by someone and wandered away. 'I saw you go very pale. Did Marcus say something to offend you?'

His mouth was very close to her ear, and she was aware of several things at once. The warmth of his arm around her waist holding her close, his strong body turned protectively towards her, his gleaming golden brown eyes tinged with concern smiling down into hers.

'No, he did not offend me.' But he had made her question if she had made the biggest mistake of her life five years ago. She searched Jed's face, her blue eyes wide and wondering. According to Marcus this stunningly handsome man she had thought she loved had wanted to marry her long ago. The man she still loved...

'Phoebe, you're very quiet.'

She lifted her hand and placed it on his chest. She caught the gleam of the gold wedding band on her finger. He covered her hand with his and she could feel the steady thud of his heart. She smiled a broad, brilliant smile. She felt the beat of his heart increase, and almost laughed out loud at her foolish plan to deny him sex as her pulse began to race.

'I was just thinking how—' She stopped. She had nearly told him she loved him. 'How pleased your father must be,' she amended swiftly, pulling her hand from beneath his as reality hit.

The shock and, yes, the euphoria brought on by Marcus's statement had blinded her for a moment to the truth. Jed had been going to marry her five years ago—but only because she'd been pregnant, not because he'd loved her, and he had married her now because of Ben. Not much had changed except that she knew Jed had definitely never suggested a termination—and she had acknowledged that anyway. She also knew he had not abandoned her either... He had been stuck here in this hospital with his father, then as now...

She recalled when Jed had discovered Ben was his and said they should marry. She had responded that he would never be anything but a part-time father. He had asked her to give him a chance, saying that he might surprise her. Well, they were married now. Perhaps it was time to give Jed, the man she had loved to hate for so long, that chance—and herself as well, because she still loved him and always would...

Jed felt the sudden tension in her, saw her brilliant smile dim, and knew that whatever she had been going to say had nothing to do with his father. How Phoebe's mind worked was a mystery to him. She was the most exasperating woman on the planet, and the most exquisite, and she was his wife...

He tightened his arm around her waist. 'It is time we left,' he said firmly.

Phoebe glanced around, her decision made. She was going to try and make a go of this marriage. Maybe there would be another baby, and maybe in time Jed would change and grow to love her... She looked up at him. 'If you say so,' she agreed, 'But what about all these people?'

'They can take care of themselves. In the circumstances no one is expecting a party,' he said dryly.

He said their goodbyes and told Cora they would be gone for the night, and to call if he was needed. With his arm still firmly fixed around her, he led her out of the room.

'Wait a minute—what do you mean, we will be away for the night?'

Ben and Cora's children were at the Sabbides house, with Maria and Cora's nanny taking care of them—but not for the whole night.

'I have to get back for Ben.'

'No, you don't. He will be perfectly well taken care of,' he said, striding along the corridor and out on to the street.

'But I've never left Ben overnight!' she exclaimed.

'Then it is time you did,' Jed drawled, and opened the door of a low-slung sports car. He saw her fastened in before sliding into the driving seat. 'We have just been married, remember?' he mocked 'Much as I love Ben, I have no intention of spending my wedding night with him.'

'Ben will miss me. I can't leave him—and anyway I have no clothes,' she declared.

'He won't… You can… And you don't need any clothes.' He grinned. 'By the way, I love the dress—it displays your legs to spectacular advantage.' He laughed as hastily she grabbed the hem and tried to pull it down to her knees.

Phoebe gave up and closed her eyes. The day had started with Jed telling Ben they were getting married. Her son had been delighted… Then Cora and her children had descended and chaos had reigned. A selection of dresses had appeared in her bedroom—all white. She'd chosen the plainest one, strapless, with a boned bodice and a short skirt that ended a good four inches above her knees. The saving grace was that there was a matching edge-to-edge crystal-trimmed coat, so she didn't feel half naked.

She drew in a deep breath and opened her eyes, and saw the car had stopped. She glanced at Jed. He was unfastening the safety harness and she was acutely aware of his long, lean body, of the faint scent of his cologne mingling with the male scent of him.

'That wasn't far.'

Phoebe had made the decision to accept Jed as her husband willingly, but that did not stop her from feeling nervous. He made no response, simply slid out of the car and walked around the front to open her door and help her out.

'Where are we?' She glanced around. A few blocks away she could see the striking outline of the Acropolis. She turned to Jed. 'We are in the middle of Athens.' She answered her own question. 'That's the Acropolis.' She pointed excitedly.

'Got it in one, Phoebe.' Jed grinned. Her pleasure in seeing the monument made him realise how little Phoebe had seen of the world. 'We are staying in my apartment tonight,' he told her as he slipped an arm around her waist and led her through some glass doors, introduced her to the doorman as his wife, and whisked her into an elevator. 'Once my father is out of danger I will take you sightseeing,' he drawled huskily.

'I'd like that.' She smiled up at him, and he had never known a ride so slow. When the doors slid open he hurried her along the hall and slid his key in the lock. He opened the door and, swinging her up in his arms, carried her inside.

'What the—?' Phoebe wrapped her arms around his neck. 'Are you crazy? Put me down!' she cried as her high-heel shoes fell off her feet.

'Crazy for you, Phoebe,' Jed drawled, closing the door with his back and walking through the hall, the vast expanse of the living area and straight into his bedroom. He was so strung out it took all his considerable self-control not to throw her on the bed and leap on her.

'Oh, my—rose petals!' Phoebe murmured, and Jed almost lost it when her lips touched his ear. He glanced around in a daze, wondering what she was talking about, and saw his very masculine bed made up with white linen and covered in rose petals. Cora's doing, no doubt, but he was not a man to miss an opportunity...

'Especially for you,' he husked, and lowered her down.

The brush of her body against his as he set her on her feet was a sweet agony.

CHAPTER TWELVE

PHOEBE looked up at Jed, her blue eyes sparkling with humor. 'I never had you pegged as the romantic rose petal type.'

She shook her head, and he was stunned by the brilliance of the smile she gave him. He made a mental note to give Cora something fabulous and tell her to keep quiet.

Jed laughed softly. 'I am not—but for you…' He trailed off throatily and slipped his hands beneath the light coat, easing it from her shoulders to drop it to the floor.

A warm tide of colour washed over Phoebe's face. The fact that he had thought of the roses beguiled her, and her nervousness vanished along with her clothes as Jed's hand reached round her back and unzipped her dress, peeled it down her body until it fell at her feet and did the same with the frill of white that passed as her briefs. He dropped to his knees to lift each foot and remove the scrap of lace.

She heard his sharp indrawn breath as he straightened up, and felt his eyes on her. His glittering gaze roved over her face and lower, to her high firm breasts, the small waist, the pale curls shielding her femininity, slowly down her long legs and finally back to her face. He reached for her, cupping her face in his hand. 'Phoebe—my beautiful bride.'

He brushed his lips lightly against hers, threading his

hands through her hair. He removed the clip she wore and smoothed the silken mass down over her shoulders and kissed her again, his hands stroking down her slender arms, and settling on her waist while his mouth worked its magic on her senses

A soft sigh of pleasure escaped her and she swayed weakly towards him, reaching for his broad shoulders. Suddenly she was swept of her feet again and placed gently in the middle of the wide bed scattered with petals.

He straightened up. 'Never have I seen anything so perfect as you.' His deep husky voice was almost reverent, and as she watched he stripped off his clothes in seconds.

'Ohhh!' She drew in a deep breath as she stared at his tall bronzed body, all taut muscle and sinew and mightily aroused. And then he lowered his long body on the bed, supporting his weight on one elbow, curving his hand round her throat, his dark gaze roaming over her.

'You are exquisite, Phoebe,' he husked, looking into her sparkling blue eyes. 'And at last you are mine—my wife,' he declared possessively, and she didn't argue.

His thumb and finger trailed down her throat and lower, until his palm cupped her breast and his fingers rubbed gently at the nipples. 'Ahhh…' she breathed as his teasing fingers excited her. Her eyes, wide and luminous, scanned his darkly handsome face and, reaching up, she ran her fingers though the silken black hair of his head.

Jed groaned and his mouth found hers in a soft caress, his tongue seeking, tasting, his hands gliding, stroking over her trembling body as he kissed her with an ever deepening passion that sparked an answering passion in her.

She felt the blood flow thicker though her veins as he lifted his head and trailed kisses down her neck, her breasts, capturing a pouting nipple between his teeth to lick and suck until she cried out at the fierce pleasure he created.

With a husky growl he retuned to her mouth and kissed her with a savage need that melted her bones. She felt the power of his muscular body against her, the caress of his strong hands sliding over her heated skin. Time ceased to exist…she was drowning in a sea of sensations so intense nothing else mattered.

She writhed beneath him as his hand traced down her stomach to settle between her thighs, his long fingers finding the small point of pleasure while his mouth and tongue and teeth explored every pulse-point with an erotic expertise that drove her wild.

Her arms wound round him as he moved between her thighs, nudging her legs apart. She heard him murmuring husky foreign sounds, and then he was there where she needed him to be, thrusting slowly, deeply, into her hot slick centre. Lost in the throes of passion, Phoebe arched up to him, her hands clasping his shoulders, his neck, any part of him she could cling to. His hands grasped her buttocks, lifting her higher, driving her higher with long deep strokes, filling her, stretching her, then slowing, twisting, teasing with short sharp strokes, and plunging deep again, then stilling.

Quivering on the brink, she looked into his molten black eyes, blazing with desire, his face taut with the effort to control his passion. The heady scent of sex and roses filled the air, and Phoebe's inner muscles flexed and clenched around him. With a low groan he thrust again, fast and firm. Phoebe cried out as her body began to convulse in climax, and she felt his body tighten, muscles locked for one long moment, and then Jed finally let go of his superhuman control and joined her, filled her with a power that went on and on in orgasmic ecstasy. She clung to him, his great body shuddering, his chest heaving, until finally he collapsed across her, his head buried in the tangled mass of her hair spread on the pillow.

Her body still quivering, she lay with her arm around his back, holding him, loving him. She felt him roll off her to lie flat on his back and her eyes fluttered closed, her breathing heavy, her body finally spent.

Later—how much later she had no idea—his strong hand stroked over her stomach and around her side to pull her close against his hard body.

'Now you really are my wife,' Jed murmured. 'But just to make sure...' And she felt his lips brush her neck and nuzzle her ear, and the magic started all over again...and again...as they rediscovered the wild, wanton passion of their past with a fervour that exhausted them both.

Phoebe opened her eyes, yawned and looked around. Jed was sprawled flat on his back beside her, one long arm stretched across the pillow above her head, the other lying at a right angle to his body, palm up. He was totally relaxed. Tentatively she moved to lean on an elbow and look down at him. His black hair curled across his brow, his long sooty eyelashes rested on the blades of his cheeks, his chiselled lips were slightly parted and he was deeply asleep.

Somehow he looked younger, the lines of strain around his mouth and eyes smoother—more like the man she'd first met and fallen in love with. Her husband, she thought with a thrill. Her gaze dropped lower to his muscular chest, and a smile twitched her lips at the rose petal stuck to his flat stomach. A sheet across his lean hips was concealing the rest of his body. She was about to reach and remove the petal, but stopped.

Jed had been awake for the past forty-eight hours— longer, in fact. It was amazing he'd had the stamina to make love at all, she thought wonderingly, never mind as many times as they had. She decided to let him sleep—he needed the rest... Sliding her legs off the bed, she silently collected her discarded clothes from the floor and entered the bathroom. She washed and cleaned her teeth—she did not want to turn on the shower in case she disturbed Jed. She filled a glass with water and drank it, then finding a comb tidied her hair. Not wanting to wear the same briefs, she popped them in the wash basket and pulled on her dress.

Carrying her coat, she tiptoed through the bedroom and into the hall to explore. She looked into the kitchen—all black and stainless steel. It looked immaculate and unused... She wandered into the living area that in the light of day looked big and surprisingly comfortable, with a big cream hide seating unit centred around a long low table, She was drawn towards the glass patio doors the length of the room, which looked out over the balcony and the city, with a superb view of the Acropolis.

She lingered awhile, simply looking, then continued her exploration and found another bedroom. She walked into the last room—what she supposed was a study, but looked more like the flight deck of a spaceship.

Two walls were lined with flashing screens—it looked like Jed's own personal stock exchange. Another had a well-used squashy cushioned slate-grey sofa pushed against it, and centre stage was a massive desk, with two computers on top and a large chair behind it.

Then she spied something else, and stood transfixed. In the middle of the desk was an open box containing the gold seal she had given Jed for his thirtieth birthday, Jed had kept her present and she felt her heart lift. His wonderful lovemaking apart, it was the first positive sign she had that he actually cared. He might never love her, but with

Ben and perhaps other children their marriage could be a success. Maybe she would not be deliriously happy, but she would settle for contentment.

Her heart and mind at last in perfect accord, she spun on her heel—and stopped as Jed appeared in the doorway.

His head was down, his shoulders hunched. Wearing a navy towelling robe, he looked like a man with the weight of the world on his shoulders.

'Are you all right?' she asked.

Jed jerked his head back, stunned by the sound of Phoebe's voice.

He had woken up feeling wonderful, after the greatest night of his life, and had turned to the source of his happiness—Phoebe. His body had been stirring in anticipation, but he had found the other side of the bed empty and cold. He'd sat up and looked around, seen his clothes still scattered on the floor but swiftly registered there was no sign of Phoebe's. For only the second time in his adult life he had panicked. He had leapt out of bed and looked in the bathroom, but there had been no sign of her ever being there. He'd pulled on a robe and returned to the bedroom, called her name. He'd stood still as a statue and listened, but the apartment had been eerily silent. She had gone...

Like a lightning bolt from the gods it had hit him. He loved Phoebe...he always had. It had never been just sex with Phoebe. No woman had ever made him feel the way she did or ever would, and he could not face losing her again.

'Phoebe. You are still here... I was frightened you had left,' Jed said hoarsely.

Wide-eyed, Phoebe stared at him. 'Whatever gave you that idea? Of course I am still here. We got married yesterday, remember?' she prompted, suddenly beginning to really worry as he staggered over to the sofa and sat down, burying his head in his hands. 'You have never been frightened in your life.' She tried to lighten the atmosphere, crossing to where he sat.

Jed was a typical Alpha male—fearless in everything he did. It was what made him so powerful and so desirable. She stopped in front of him, and he looked up, and she noticed his ashen face. The glittering eyes were not feral, but full of what looked suspiciously like deep pain, and suddenly she was afraid.

'Has something happened? Is it your father or Ben?'

'No, nothing like that,' he said swiftly, and reached for her hand. He took it in his, his fingers linking with hers. She tried to pull free. 'No—please, Phoebe, let me explain.'

He looked so different, so vulnerable—not the hard, arrogant man she was accustomed to. She was intrigued— and he *had* said please...

A gentle tug on her hand and she sat down beside him. 'This had better be good, Jed. I want to go and see Ben soon.' He turned, his knee touching her leg, and clasped her hand tightly in his on his thigh, looking down as if seeking inspiration, then back to her face.

'I woke up this morning and turned to hold you. You were not there. I looked in the bathroom, and then I noticed my clothes were still strewn around the room but yours had gone. I know this sounds chauvinistic, but in the past when we spent the night together you would never have picked up your clothes and left mine.'

Phoebe smiled. 'You're right—it is chauvinistic.'

'Then it hit me. You had left—run away again—and I love you,' he said hoarsely.

Jed had said he loved her—words she had longed to hear for so very long—and she couldn't believe it. She studied his handsome features, saw the strain in his dark eyes. But… 'I don't believe you.'

'I don't blame you. I know I treated you abominably in the past—and in the present. Maybe I should start at the beginning.' He sounded uncertain—a first for Jed, Phoebe thought. 'But please listen,' he pleaded. 'If I don't tell you now I might never have the nerve again.'

'All right, I'm listening,' she encouraged.

'I have loved you from the moment I saw you, Phoebe, but in my conceit I took your innocence, your love for granted, without giving anything in return.'

'Not true. You gave me rather a lot of jewellery,' she prompted.

'Exactly—something that cost me nothing in relation to my wealth and, as you so rightly said, was sleazy. But I never saw it like that. I only had to look at you to want you—still do.' He tried to smile. 'The months we were together were the happiest of my life—until tragedy struck and I handled it very badly. I thought only of myself, not how you were feeling. But I never meant to leave you. My father had a heart attack.'

'I know—Marcus told me,' she murmured.

'Yes, well…you can't use a cellphone in Intensive Care, so I gave mine to Christina and told her to call you and tell you I'd be delayed.'

'She didn't call me. I called her,' Phoebe said. 'She was very sympathetic and told me she was used to getting rid of your women. She said you had told her to inform me you were not coming back, and advised me to leave.'

'She *what*?' One ebony brow arched in outrage. 'She never got rid of a woman for me in her life—I got rid of *her*, four years ago, when I belatedly realised she wanted to be more than my PA. And I certainly never asked her to tell you to leave, she told me you *wanted* to go.'

'Going over the past is pointless,' Phoebe said with a shake of her head. 'Let's be honest—you could have found me if you had really wanted to. You had no trouble finding me last week,' she said bluntly. 'Marcus also told me you wanted to marry me before, but we both know it would not have been for love but because of the baby—the same as now.' She wasn't going to trust his avowal of love so easily.

'I deserve that, but it isn't the real truth.' His dark eyes held hers. There was vulnerability in the black depths, and his complexion was deepening into what looked rather like a blush. 'I didn't look for you because I was an emotional coward. When I returned to the apartment and you had gone I told myself it was for the best that you had moved on, because it meant I did not have to face how I really felt. I also felt guilty because you had lost the baby.'

'You felt guilty?' Phoebe queried. 'Why?'

'For the first time in my adult life I panicked when you told me you were pregnant. When I got over the shock I knew I wanted to marry you, but I'm ashamed to say I was in no hurry to tell you. Then, when I got to the hospital and the doctor told me you had lost the baby, he also gave me a few words of caution. He said he had noticed bruises on your thighs and a few other places, and that it would be a good idea to tone down the sex a little—especially if you got pregnant again. He said I could go in and see you. I walked into your room, totally disgusted with myself and feeling as guilty as hell. *I* might have caused you to lose the baby.'

Phoebe's head was reeling. His confession had come totally out of the blue. The look of disgust on his face as he had entered her hospital room had haunted her for years, but it had never been for her, as she'd thought, but at himself. A spark of hope ignited in her heart. Maybe he did love her.

Suddenly she was incensed on Jed's behalf. 'The doctor should never have told you that. The way we made love had nothing to do with him, and I enjoyed every minute. It certainly was not your fault I lost the baby.'

For a second his eyes sparkled with a trace of his usual arrogance. 'Maybe not, but along with Christina's meddling it gave me another convenient excuse for not trying to find you. Because, being honest, I realised it was a relief as well. I always like to be in control, and what I felt for you terrified me. Our relationship was the longest I had ever had—I only had to think of you to want you with an ache that would not go away. I told myself it was lust, but deep down I knew I lied. I loved everything about you— your breathtaking smile, your quick enquiring mind.' His piercing black eyes seemed to see right into her soul. 'The soft avowals of love you gave so freely. I'd give anything to hear them again.'

Phoebe gave him a tentative smile, but still wasn't sure she believed him.

'I panicked for the second time in my life this morning, when I woke and you were gone. But this time for a different reason.' His hands tightened on hers and she stared up at him. The planes and angles of his face were taut, and she wondered what was coming next to make him so tense. 'Because I finally admitted to myself that I love you, Phoebe, and only you. I could not bear the thought of losing you—I could not go through that pain again.'

He let go of her hands, and leaning over her, clasped her face between his palms. His black eyes looked deep into her wary blue.

'You have to believe me, Phoebe. I love you.' He shook his head slightly and a black curl fell over his brow. She

lifted her hand to sweep it away but then dropped it again.
'I never even looked at another woman for over two years
after you left.' His hands slid down to her shoulders, his
fingers flexing in her bare skin, and she shivered but Jed
did not seem to notice.

'That I find hard to believe,' she murmured. Jed was
a highly-sexed man, but she was flattered at the thought,
and the spark of hope burned brighter with every word he
said.

'It is absolutely true, I swear, but I know you don't trust
me—how could you after the way I behaved? The moment
I saw you at the embassy I was determined to get you back.
I could have flattened Gladstone when he kissed you.'

She recognised the green devil in his eyes. 'That is all
Julian ever did,' she told him. Honesty cut both ways.

'Thank you for that,' he acknowledged, and continued,
'The day I found out about Ben I was angry and I blamed
you, but it was my own fault because I had wasted five
years denying how I truly felt. I could not resist making
love to you the same night. Phoebe, I know I don't deserve
you, and I am not asking you to love me—only to stay
with me and let me love and care for you. Please give me
another chance.'

Phoebe lifted her hand, and this time she did sweep the
black curl back from his brow. Jed pleading for her love
was something she had never imagined, and her heart was
filled with love. But did she trust him?

'I said my father was a silly old fool for keeping his
promise to my mother. But now I know exactly how he
feels. I love you, I adore you, I worship the ground you
walk on—and I am the bigger fool for being an abject
coward and not admitting it sooner. And if the answer is
no—' his hands tightened on her shoulders and he looked
like a man going to the gallows '—I will give you and Ben

your freedom. You can return to England and I will be a visiting father.' He grimaced. 'Like you said, some things are unconscionable and I can do no less.'

'You won't have to.' She took a leap of faith and trusted Jed with her heart. 'I do love you, Jed, and always have,' Phoebe said, her eyes inexplicably filling with tears as elation flooded through her. She gave him a beautiful smile. Jed loved her. Her husband—the magnificent man she had thought emotionless—loved her. He had done all along, but had been too afraid to admit his feelings. 'If you remember, I used to tell you so all the time—too naive to hide my feelings,' she declared, and it was there for him to see in the brilliant blue eyes blazing into his. 'Nothing has changed, I love you and always will…'

'Ah, Phoebe. If only you knew how I have longed to hear you say those words again,' Jed murmured throatily, and he kissed her almost reverently, with love and a deep, soulful passion that touched her heart and melted her bones.

A long moment later he lifted his head. 'You have made me the happiest man alive.' He looked into her gleaming blue eyes, his own burning black. 'Do you remember you once gave me a gold heart? Well, I have cherished it for years. It is my lucky charm and it always gave me hope.'

'Of course I remember. I just saw it on your desk and it gave *me* hope simply knowing you had kept it,' Phoebe said softly.

He smiled and kissed her brow. 'Now you have gifted me your true heart, and for that I am eternally grateful. I will love, cherish and protect you till my dying day.' He kissed her again.

In moments she was beneath him, his robe shrugged off and her dress removed. Naked, he smiled down at her, his eyes full of humor and love. 'Now for the worship and adoration,' he murmured.

They made love with a slow, aching tenderness, stroking, sighing and murmuring soft words of love and need. And finally, when the passion built to fever pitch, Jed thrust into her sleek, welcoming body and they came together in a meeting of body and mind—two soul mates becoming one in a wild, wonderful climax.

'What is it with you and sofas?' Phoebe teased when she finally got her breath back. She lifted her hand to run her fingers gently down his cheek and then curved her slender arm lovingly around his neck.

Jed kissed her lightly on the lips. 'The place does not matter. All that really matters is that I am with you, Phoebe—the woman I love with all my heart, now and always.'

EPILOGUE

'TALK about a big Greek wedding—this is incredible.' Phoebe turned laughing eyes up to her husband. 'Have you seen your father and Aunt Jemma dancing with the children?'

Jed glanced across the crowded ballroom and spotted the older couple. He turned back to his wife. 'If he didn't have a bad heart to start with Jemma would give him one,' he stated with a broad grin.

Phoebe looked radiant. He had not the words to do justice to her beauty, inside and out. Her hair, pale as moonlight, was swept up in an intricate loop on the top of her head to cascade in a shimmering silken swathe down her back. The long dress she wore fitted her shapely body like a glove. White satin and embroidered with Swarovski crystals, it sparkled as she moved—but not half as much as his fabulous wife did in his eyes. Jed had insisted on a church wedding, and the white dress, to show the world his virgin bride.

Phoebe would call him a chauvinist if she knew, but it gave him immense pride and satisfaction to know he was the only man who had ever made love to her or ever would, he silently vowed. She was the love of his life… She was his life—he'd be lost without her.

'Are you enjoying yourself? Not the nightmare you

envisaged?' he asked, tightening his arm around her waist and smiling down at her.

'Yes, the church service was beautiful—and I actually understood what the priest said this time.' Phoebe laughed. 'You were right,' she conceded to her husband.

But then Jed was always right. He had insisted on the big wedding, the same as he had insisted on her Aunt Jemma, after she came back from Australia, coming to stay with them in Greece for a few weeks. Now, apart from the odd trip back to England, her aunt spent all her time here.

One year had passed since Ben had met his father, and now he spoke Greek like a native and loved his big Greek family and friends. Phoebe loved everyone—but especially her husband. With every day that passed their love got stronger, and Marcus had been right when he'd said Jed's emotions ran deep. Her indomitable husband had opened up to her in a way she would never have thought possible a year ago. He had actually cried at the arrival of the latest additions to their family. That he loved her she had no doubt, and she would trust him with her life.

Reaching up, she ran her fingers through his hair and kissed him.

'I love you, wife,' Jed murmured when they came up for air. 'Let's leave now, and I'll show you how much.'

Phoebe pulled back. 'I love you too, husband.' A slow, sensuous smile curved her lips, and there was a wicked gleam in her blue eyes. 'But now you have the heir, the spare *and* the bonus. I'm not sure we should,' she teased him. 'Don't you dare, Jed,' she said as he hauled her close.

He had laughed when she told him about the no-sex plan she'd had on marrying him. And he'd been stunned when she hadn't told him until she was over three months that she was pregnant again because she hadn't wanted him getting paranoid about their love-life—he was such an over-protective husband.

She had confessed she had conceived that night they had met again, explaining at his surprise that she had not wanted to look a fool by admitting she hadn't taken the pill since they'd parted—telling him she had not needed to because she had never had another lover. He had been humbled and overwhelmed with love. She never ceased to amaze him—no more so than three months ago, when she had given birth to a set of healthy twins—a boy, Leo, and a girl, Leanne. He had openly wept.

Phoebe—his wife, the mother of his children—filled his heart and his life with so much love and joy that he thanked God every day that he had found her.

But sometimes a man had to be a man. And, sweeping her up in his arms, he carried her out of the ballroom—to the cheers and laughter of the family and all their guests.

Coming Next Month

from **Harlequin Presents® EXTRA.** Available November 9, 2010.

Coming Next Month

from **Harlequin Presents®.** Available November 23, 2010.

LARGER-PRINT BOOKS!

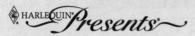

GET 2 FREE LARGER-PRINT
NOVELS PLUS 2 FREE GIFTS!

YES! Please send me 2 FREE LARGER-PRINT Harlequin Presents® novels and my 2 FREE gifts (gifts are worth about $10). After receiving them, if I don't wish to receive any more books, I can return the shipping statement marked "cancel". If I don't cancel, I will receive 6 brand-new novels every month and be billed just $4.55 per book in the U.S. or $5.24 per book in Canada. That's a saving of at least 13% off the cover price! It's quite a bargain! Shipping and handling is just 50¢ per book.* I understand that accepting the 2 free books and gifts places me under no obligation to buy anything. I can always return a shipment and cancel at any time. Even if I never buy another book, the two free books and gifts are mine to keep forever.

176/376 HDN E5NG

Name	(PLEASE PRINT)	
Address		Apt. #
City	State/Prov.	Zip/Postal Code

Signature (if under 18, a parent or guardian must sign)

Mail to the **Harlequin Reader Service:**
IN U.S.A.: P.O. Box 1867, Buffalo, NY 14240-1867
IN CANADA: P.O. Box 609, Fort Erie, Ontario L2A 5X3

Not valid for current subscribers to Harlequin Presents Larger-Print books.

**Are you a subscriber to Harlequin Presents books
and want to receive the larger-print edition?
Call 1-800-873-8635 today!**

* Terms and prices subject to change without notice. Prices do not include applicable taxes. Sales tax applicable in N.Y. Canadian residents will be charged applicable provincial taxes and GST. Offer not valid in Quebec. This offer is limited to one order per household. All orders subject to approval. Credit or debit balances in a customer's account(s) may be offset by any other outstanding balance owed by or to the customer. Please allow 4 to 6 weeks for delivery. Offer available while quantities last.

Your Privacy: Harlequin Books is committed to protecting your privacy. Our Privacy Policy is available online at www.eHarlequin.com or upon request from the Reader Service. From time to time we make our lists of customers available to reputable third parties who may have a product or service of interest to you. If you would prefer we not share your name and address, please check here. ☐

Help us get it right—We strive for accurate, respectful and relevant communications. To clarify or modify your communication preferences, visit us at www.ReaderService.com/consumerschoice.

HPLP10R

HARLEQUIN®

A Romance

FOR EVERY MOOD™

Spotlight on

Classic

Quintessential, modern love stories
that are romance at its finest.

See the next page
to enjoy a sneak peek from
the Harlequin® Romance series.

*See below for a sneak peek from our classic
Harlequin® Romance® line.*

Introducing DADDY BY CHRISTMAS by Patricia Thayer.

M<small>IA</small> caught sight of Jarrett when he walked into the open lobby. It was hard not to notice the man. In a charcoal business suit with a crisp white shirt and striped tie covered by a dark trench coat, he looked more Wall Street than small-town Colorado.

Mia couldn't blame him for keeping his distance. He was probably tired of taking care of her.

Besides, why would a man like Jarrett McKane be interested in her? Why would he want to take on a woman expecting a baby? Yet he'd done so many things for her. He'd been there when she'd needed him most. How could she not care about a man like that?

Heart pounding in her ears, she walked up behind him. Jarrett turned to face her. "Did you get enough sleep last night?"

"Yes, thanks to you," she said, wondering if he'd thought about their kiss. Her gaze went to his mouth, then she quickly glanced away. "And thank you for not bringing up my meltdown."

Jarrett couldn't stop looking at Mia. Blue was definitely her color, bringing out the richness of her eyes.

"What meltdown?" he said, trying hard to focus on what she was saying. "You were just exhausted from lack of sleep and worried about your baby."

He couldn't help remembering how, during the night, he'd kept going in to watch her sleep. How strange was that? "I hope you got enough rest."

She nodded. "Plenty. And you're a good neighbor for

coming to my rescue."

He tensed. Neighbor? *What neighbor kisses you like I did?* "That's me, just the full-service landlord," he said, trying to keep the sarcasm out of his voice. He started to leave, but she put her hand on his arm.

"Jarrett, what I meant was you went beyond helping me." Her eyes searched his face. "I've asked far too much of you."

"Did you hear me complain?"

She shook her head. "You should. I feel like I've taken advantage."

"Like I said, I haven't minded."

"And I'm grateful for everything…"

Grasping her hand on his arm, Jarrett leaned forward. The memory of last night's kiss had him aching for another. "I didn't do it for your gratitude, Mia."

Gorgeous tycoon Jarrett McKane has never believed in Christmas—but he can't help being drawn to soon-to-be-mom Mia Saunders! Christmases past were spent alone…and now Jarrett may just have a fairy-tale ending for all his Christmases future!

Available December 2010,
only from Harlequin® Romance®.